Contents

Robert Westall

Love Match

mammoth

First published in Great Britain 1997
by Methuen Children's Books Ltd
Published 2000 by Mammoth
an imprint of Egmont Children's Books Limited,
a division of Egmont Holding Limited
239 Kensington High Street, London W8 6SA

Claudine © 1993 The Estate of Robert Westall
First published in Great Britain 1996 in
Heart to Heart, edited by Miriam Hodgson
The Women's Hour © 1994 The Estate of Robert Westall
First published in Great Britain 1994 in
In Between, edited by Miriam Hodgson

ISBN 0 7497 3097 8

10 9 8 7 6 5 4 3 2 1

A CIP catalogue record for this title
is available from the British Library

Printed in Great Britain
by Cox & Wyman Ltd, Reading, Berkshire

Contents

Love Match   1

The Concert   34

The Women's Hour   49

Claudine   61

Lulworth Cove   102

Fatty France   122

First Death   164

Love Match

I learned my tennis the hard way; ten-a-side. If Becker and McEnroe think they have it tough, they don't know nothing. We didn't just have sprains and pulled thigh-muscles. Rackets clashed and exploded like fireworks; at least one every lunch-time. That was where Ricky Thomson lost four front teeth to an overhead smash; by one of his own side. People were carried off with broken arms and legs before the Head finally stopped it.

I suppose we were a pretty hard lot, for a grammar school. Garmouth *Municipal* Grammar School, and it looked it. Four storeys high. Elizabethan-style architecture in glaring red and yellow brick; pillars as graceful as milk-bottles and the legends 'Boys' and 'Girls' graven in stone over separate entrances; well, graven in glaring yellow brick, anyway. It was, in plan, like a fat-bodied 'T' with the bottom of the 'T' facing the road and the public. On one side, the boys' playground, on the other the girls'. Both playgrounds were lethally composed of slabs of concrete six feet square that had tilted over the ages, leaving half-inch edges exposed that could trip you and send you arse-over-tip. It didn't matter much with the girls, because they never moved above a prim walk, spent all their playground time in little huddles, being catty about each other and comparing their results in the maths homework. But the younger lads liked to chase and run, using innocent bystanders as turning-posts and leaving them spinning like tops under the impact of their sweaty hands. Given those half-inch steps in the concrete, the gym teacher's first-aid kit was always busy, and the hospital down the road did a roaring trade in concussion.

As you will imagine, for the younger males and females, it was a case of never the twain shall meet, outside the grim order of the class-rooms. More than a gulf separated them; two privet hedges, a row of spiked iron railings, and the window of the Head's room.

But in the sixth form, having, as the Head said (or at least hoped), matured, the sexes were allowed to mingle on the rear third play-ground. By and large, the girls stayed in their half and we in ours. But we exchanged curious stares, winks, smiles and the results of our maths homework (at which we were actually better than them, by some unlooked for miracle).

So matters stood in the two winter terms. But in the summer term, on all three playgrounds, tennis-nets appeared, and the worn-away yellow lines on the concrete achieved some significance. This made little difference during school hours in the girls' playground, though I believe they used the net to rest their maths homework on. The little lads were more creative, using the net for hurdles in their running (causing more hospitalisations if they didn't quite make it) as well as pushing each other over the net backwards or wrapping each other up in its nether folds, and leaving each other squealing helplessly when the bell went.

But on the back playground, in the lunch-time, the sixth-form boys played ten-a-side tennis. A massed rank of four up to the net, then three on the service-line and three on the base-line. The sides weren't picked, they just gathered, of people who were fool enough to use their own rackets, or had a friend who was fool enough to lend them theirs. There was no scoring; nobody wanted *scores*. The yellow lines were ignored, and there were always about six tatty ragged balls in motion at once. No, you *won* by hammering the ball as hard as you could at the face of your worst enemy, or stealing the ball off your best friend's racket, with a ferocious shout of 'MINE', or simply getting your racket between your best friend's legs as he was going full out and leaving him lying full length on the unforgiving concrete. It all got a lot of laughs. And we played, of course, in full school uniform, and shoes with steel heelcaps that struck sparks like a horse's hooves.

Why did we do it, apart from the laughs, the sarcastic shouts of, 'Well played, sir!'? I think we played to impress the girls, who gathered nervously to watch from the safety of the grassy bank that led up to the school playing-field.

Nobody ever taught me a stroke; I invented my own, in that confined scrum, for which there were no names. They would probably have had Dan Maskell foaming at the mouth (yes, he was around and already middle-aged, when I was young). But I had a good eye, and a quick body. I played rugby for the county juniors. My strokes *worked*.

Probably my tennis would have ended there, but for the day that nearly all the Sixth were away on a combined geography/biology field course. Being an English, maths and art man myself, I didn't go. And that day, when I turned up for lunch-time tennis, I found only three on the court, and two of them were on the school tennis team. Fatty Alderson and Russy Pewterspear always played doubles together, and a nastier pair never lived. They were always taking the piss out of somebody, and I *loathed* them. They were playing, that day, against David Yeoman, who was their favourite victim, their ever-present victim. For horrible though they were to him, he was always hanging around them. No beastliness on their part ever seemed to drive him away. He was an unfortunate youth, with big ears and smarmed-back honey-coloured hair, and sticky-out teeth, but otherwise quite a reasonable guy. I couldn't see what they had against him; and I couldn't see why he went on taking it from them.

Anyway, that day they were playing against him, two against one, and making him run from one side of the court to the other, and sending ball after ball past him, turning him into a panting, red-faced heap. I mean, you can beat a guy without making him look an idiot with drop shots, when, to get back your last drive, he's had to climb the coke-heap at the back of the court . . .

It made me quietly mad, so I strolled up and said off-handed, 'Mind if I join you?'

They didn't like that much; didn't like the odds being evened up, and didn't like *me*. But they couldn't say no, not with the girls watching. It would have meant no guts.

So I played. And I played in a way that, I must say, amazed even me. I mean, I'd noticed before I played a lot better when the sun was shining, and I played a lot better when I was angry, really mad.

But that day I could do nothing wrong. My great whizzing forehand, which usually hit the net, went in every shot. And my backhand, which was steadier for some reason, went in low and mean and almost turned at right-angles with the spin I was putting on it, and hardly bounced at all. And old Yeoman, suddenly glad to have a mate, began to play like a dream too. It began to be *them* who were spending half the time climbing the coke-heaps, looking for the balls. So I made the most of it.

'Play you a set?' I suddenly shouted. They couldn't, didn't dare, say no. With the girls watching, it would have been all round the school that they were scared of me, and worse, scared of Yeoman, their constant victim.

So they said yes.

They soon wished they bloody hadn't. My big serve began to go in as well, and, even worse, it kept on hitting one of those raised cracks in the playground and shooting up into the air, inaccessible till it landed on the coke-heap behind.

One of the girls, Pat Hope, came trotting across with a malicious grin on her face, and offered to act as umpire. She began keeping the score before they could say no.

Fatty and Russy really tried to fend off disgrace, but it just wasn't their day, not with all the spectators clapping our every shot and their every mistake. In the end, they even began to serve double-faults, a thing unknown.

I shouted out a little rhyme that came into my head then.

'Double, double, toil and trouble
Fatty boil and Russy bubble . . .'

Which was true enough, for Fatty was boiling with rage by that time, very red in the face, and Russy was almost crying with frustration, which in our part of the world we call 'bubbling'.

It got a big laugh from the girls. It got me the name of being a wit. It made our opponents start to quarrel with each other, also a thing unknown, till then, and in the end, to the amazement of both school and staff, we ran out winners, 6–3. The news went round like wildfire, of course; they were not popular.

They were cunning sods, though. Know what they did? They went to the sports master and recommended that I be made a reserve for the school tennis team, with Yeoman as my partner. They made it so that all the staff thought they had *discovered* me. And of course they put me in a no-win situation. If, when the time came, I played well, they got the credit. But if the sun went in, or I got in the wrong mood, and I played badly, I got the disgrace. I knew I was half a laughing-stock already, when the sports master welcomed me on to the squad.

'I'm not sure I agree with this, Tuffin,' he said. 'You have a certain *natural* ability, but your strokes are most unorthodox, and leave no margin for error. Ah, well, we shall see, we shall see . . .' and he went back to his teacher mates, grinning when he thought I couldn't see him, but I could see it reflected in his mates' faces. I mean, it was the way he had said *natural*. He made me feel like a performing chimpanzee in a circus.

But that wasn't the really important thing. The really important thing was that two girls came up to me, one after the other, when I was walking off to art lessons after finishing that set.

The first was Pat Hope, who was a pretty good tennis-player herself, on the girls' team, though she was far too pretty and flirty to really fling herself about and win championships. Her face was pink with pleasure as she said to me: 'I think you're *lovely* – those two have had it coming for a long time!'

No sooner had she stopped speaking than a taller figure loomed over her. God, it was Felicity Grayson, the girls' team captain and school champion. Who was also Head Girl and already had a scholarship to Cambridge. I mean, she was so grand and snooty she never spoke to *any* of us lads. But now her face cracked into a smile, and she looked quite human for a moment, as she said: 'Congratulations. I have never seen a backhand like yours in all my life. I doubt *I* could get it back. I must tell Dan about it, when I see him next . . .'

I glared at her, to see if she was taking the mickey. The Dan she mentioned in such a queenly way was the great Dan Maskell himself. Everyone knew she went to tennis school in the summer holidays, where he coached.

But she was smiling at me gently; it was a very nice smile. If she was taking the mickey, she was doing it very gently.

But Pat Hope gave her a glare. I remember I thought, not much love lost between those two.

I didn't know how right I was.

Now I was into tennis, really into it, I thought I'd better do things properly. I went to the Army and Navy Stores, and bought a pair of white shorts cheap. They were naval officers' tropical shorts, part of their uniform. By that time Britain had more shorts than naval officers . . . I already had a white shirt and white pumps from cricket, but I whitened the pumps with three layers of whitener, because they'd got a bit green with three years on the cricket square . . .

You mustn't think I had any illusions about my game; I did *not* think I was Geoff Brown or Budge Patty. No, I was keen to get among the girls, where I hadn't had much success up till then, mainly through giving up with them before I started, and not really trying.

You see, the only chances we had to chat up girls were either between lessons or at things like the school dance. And if you chatted them up between lessons all the other lads would be watching, and would get you in the toilets afterwards, saying things like, 'What did you speak to *that* thing for – she's got legs like bananas.' Or 'Her tits are so big she can hardly walk upright.'

And at the formal school dances, all the girls massed on one side, in their party frocks, and all the boys on the other, with their hands in their pockets to show how tough they were, and they didn't give two buggers. And to ask a girl to dance, you had to cross the great wide polished floor between. And the girl might say get lost, and then you'd have to walk all the way back to go and hide in the cloakroom while everyone else was laughing their heads off. I couldn't dance anyway, so to hell with it . . .

But two miles away, at Garmouth Park on the seafront, there were public tennis-courts, with changing-rooms and things. I mean, if you wanted to play in public, before a jeering audience of your mates, you played in the evenings. But if you wanted to play in private, there was hardly ever anybody there the rest of the day, and even then they were total strangers.

And it was OK to ask a girl to play tennis. I mean, it was just a *game*. If you didn't get on well, while you were playing, you just said, 'Ta for the match' at the end and parted for ever. But if you'd got on well, you would sit on the bench afterwards and discuss the match and admire her legs in shorts, and even hope for a glimpse of something when she unbuttoned her shirt one extra button because she was innocently hot. And if you'd got on very well indeed, you might offer her an ice from the kiosk and go and watch the little kids and old men sailing their boats on the park lake, and make witty remarks to make her laugh, and she might tell you about her kid brother, and you might end up going for a walk along the pier . . . I mean, *anything* could happen . . . but at any stage either of you could jump back if it got too much, and nobody lost any face.

Well, I was just in the early stages with a couple of girls, when I went down to the courts one morning on spec, to see if I could find anyone there who wanted a game.

And there was somebody there.

Felicity Grayson. In full tennis gear. On her own. Tapping her racket impatiently against her foot as if she couldn't wait to start playing tennis. Kept looking at her watch, too. I just knew somebody had let her down. She kept on staring along the seafront and giving delicate, ladylike sighs.

'Somebody not turned up?' I asked hopefully, at last. Drifting up to her casually, as if by accident. After I had watched her for at least quarter of an hour, and for the first time realised what pretty legs she had, and how neat her bottom and hips were, under her short tennis-skirt. I mean, until that point, she had almost been royalty to me, a mere sub-prefect. I mean, you don't lust after royalty; at least we didn't in those days.

'Rita Coulson,' she said, in a voice of total disgust. 'She sleeps in, and her mother works, and there's no one to wake her up. This is the second time this week.'

'Fancy a knock-up, while you're waiting?'

She looked at me, and I became aware I was wearing pale fawn socks, not the correct white ones. I became aware that there were threads of material fraying off the only tennis balls I had to play with, whereas hers were nearly new and people said she got them second-hand from Wimbledon . . .

'All right,' she said grudgingly, and went down the steps to the court, with me following, looking at the neat white parting on top of her head and smelling her faint sweet perfume, and realising that a tennis champion, a Head Girl, a coming Cambridge undergraduate, could still be a very attractive female.

It didn't help my game. Nor did the grey sky. I got worse and worse, until she said, 'Heavens, I thought you could *play*,' and made the mistake of looking at her watch.

My next forehand whizzed past her nose before she could get her racket up. Three backhands crossed the net-cord like arrows, right into the far corner of the court, leaving her gasping and floundering like a landed codfish.

Then she settled down to tame me. We didn't play games; we didn't keep the score. We just belted the hell out of each other, in long, hair-raising rallies, till the park-keeper came and yelled down through the wire that our time was up and we'd had twenty extra minutes and did we want to pay for another hour?

We flopped on to the bench side by side, steaming hot. Funny, getting hot loosens girls up. They glow; they flop most attractively. Even Head Girls undo shirt buttons, and have lace on their bras.

'You don't keep your eye on the ball long enough,' she said, wiping her red face on an immaculately clean towel. 'It would improve your strokes if you watched the ball right on to the racket head. You could be quite good, if you had coaching . . .'

'I had an hour's coaching off Reg the Legs,' I said (he was our sports master). 'It put me off me game for a week. I'm just a *natural*.'

She flicked up her eyes, at my imitation of Reg, and laughed. Her eyes were large, brown flecked with gold, and really friendly. Her teeth were white and small and very even. Her dark hair was long and glossy and lay on her white-shirted shoulders, and I wanted to run my fingers through it, even if it was a bit wet with sweat.

'Would you like an ice-cream?' I asked. I mean, I actually had the effrontery to ask. It felt nearly as subversive as asking Princess Elizabeth to go to the pictures behind Prince Philip's back.

But she didn't exactly rush to say no. Even though she knew what it meant. Then she nodded at me gravely, and blushed a little, and said, 'Yes, please.' And I realised she was lonely. I realised you can climb so high, win so many of this world's prizes that you really have no friends left. And a Head Girl can't afford to be human like the rest of us, and get herself gossiped about. That little glimpse of the real her made me feel very privileged and very protective.

We walked around the lake and watched the small boys and old men sailing their yachts.

We even walked along the pier. And she not only told me about her kid brother, but her mother and father, and her taste in jazz.

We had the same taste in jazz. Neither of us liked family outings in the car on Sunday afternoons. Neither of us liked shellfish.

I had this mad idea that we were made for each other.

But it all ended at the bus-stop for home. The gulf yawned; real life reasserted its horrible self. She would go off and things would just slide back to normal. This wonderful morning was all I was ever going to have of her.

And yet, she seemed reluctant, strangely reluctant, to get aboard the bus. Even when the driver got aboard and started revving up his engine and changing the destination-board . . . even when the conductor yelled at her, 'Come on, love, if you're coming . . .'

She gave me one beseeching look, as she reluctantly got on the back platform and reached into her purse for her fare. And finally, dumb me, I realised she was waiting to be asked out again.

'Same time tomorrow?' I shouted, as the bus roared away, drowning my voice.

But she heard me. Her whole face lit up with a smile, and she waved as urgently and long as if she were on a ship leaving dock on long voyage.

That was the beginning of the happy time. After A levels, the long summer holidays stretched ahead. And, on the empty courts of Garmouth Park, all the lovely empty mornings were ours.

Of course, she learned to cope with my sneaky strokes; she was good. And the tarmac court left me no nasty cracks to hit with my service. But my game improved too; because she kept on shouting gently, 'Watch the ball! Right till you hit it!'

We had some good tussles, but she usually won 6–4 or 6–3. She said it was good to understand the way I played my shots; she would even mimic them, gently, and I recognised myself and was reduced to hoots of laughter.

But it was her I loved, more than the tennis. Her tall, queenly grace; her slight gangliness because her legs were so long. And the way she showed her knickers when she leaned over the net to retrieve the balls. It wasn't a matter of lust, unless lust is a soft, warm, sadness better than happiness, an urge to cherish. She reminded me, doing that, of how she must have looked when she was nine.

There wasn't a lot of sexiness in any of it; partly because we only

13

met in the mornings, in a public park, and there was never anywhere private to go, except the empty morning pier, where any passing ship, or any bird-watcher with binoculars on the cliffs had us in full view. But there was walking along with our bare, warm arms twined about three times round each other, and sometimes our twined hands would bang against her bottom, and I would feel her whole body vibrate. And we kissed, of course, behind the lighthouse at the end of the pier, away from land, having made sure that no ships full of lecherous Norwegian sailors were passing. I don't think she'd ever kissed anybody before; the first time she kept her lips pressed tight together; but she kissed me so hard I thought my teeth would cave in. We soon got better, and learned to turn our heads so that our noses didn't collide. We also tried rubbing noses, to find out what Eskimos saw in it; it was quite pleasant, but we didn't make a habit of it . . .

There was only one bad moment. The morning we were on the court and couldn't hide in time, and Fatty and Russy turned up. There was nothing we could do except hit the ball as hard as possible at each other, to show near-dislike.

They watched us from behind the wire for some time, in silence. Then I heard Russy say, 'D'you think they're going together?' in a very evil, speculative voice.

Fatty considered a long time. Then he said sagely, 'Nah. She's just getting ready for the tournament. All the top females at Wimbledon practise against fellers. Fellers hit the ball harder. She's a cunning bitch. If she practised against the top girls, they'd get to know all her little new tricks.'

'Yeah,' said Russy, very discouraged; and having made a few snide remarks on our worst strokes, they drifted off to torment somebody else.

We breathed a sigh of relief, and had a good laugh over it afterwards. And yet their remarks stuck in my mind, like a tiny barbed hook. For the tournament was coming up, second week of the holidays. The Garmouth Tennis Club Tournament. Garmouth Tennis Club was very, very posh and wealthy, and lived in a private park called Prior's Park. You had to live in posh Prior Terrace before you were allowed in. Their white buildings and smooth green courts seemed to me in those days nearly as grand as Wimbledon. Those courts were as much superior to the public tarmac courts as the public courts were above the terrible school courts. They had scoreboards like Wimbledon.

And every year they held a schools tournament for the best players of all the schools around. Invitation only.

There was a boys' singles, with thirty-two entries; same with the girls. I knew I hadn't a prayer of being asked. The winners would be practically the junior champions of Garside, and the coach for the county junior team would be there to watch.

But the mixed doubles, that was different. They were the light relief, more a social occasion. Established players invited their boyfriends or girlfriends, if they were any good at tennis at all. All very relaxed. And I was sure, poor deluded fool that I was, that Felicity would invite me. I vowed I wouldn't let her down. We might even win . . . not that I cared much about that. I just wanted to be with her. And I wanted to show the world suddenly that we *were* a couple.

I waited till the last day of the school term for her to ask me. I wasn't going to be seeing her for a week, because she was going on holiday with her family to Bournemouth. I remember we were standing side by side on the grass slope above the back court at school, watching the peasants still trying to kill each other at ten-a-side. I'd long since given that up. Now my tennis-racket was important to me; I didn't want to risk breaking it, 'cos I couldn't afford a new one. Besides, you have to grow up sometime.

It was nearly bell-time, and still she hadn't asked me. I grew desperate.

'Shall we play a week come Monday?' I said, finally. 'We'll have to talk tactics for the tournament . . .'

She turned to me, baffled. 'Tournament? You want to come? I can get you a seat, if you want to watch me. I just thought you'd be bored, sitting watching all day.' Yes, she looked baffled, but suddenly she looked guilty too.

'The mixed doubles,' I said, still all trusting.

'I'm playing with Gordon Graham. From Whitley Bay Grammar. Daddy arranged it. Gordon's their champion this year. My father knows his father at the Tennis Club.'

I knew Gordon Graham. He played rugby against us, and I had taken a great delight in flattening him the last time our teams met. A blond Adonis, curly hair and a profile like a Greek god, and his jeweller father had just bought him a second-hand MG sports car. Nobody liked him much, except the girls. The boys thought he had the biggest head in the world.

'Bloody hell,' I said. 'You're not playing with that drip?'

She bridled. 'He's a very nice boy. I've known him all my life. We used to play together as kids.'

Suddenly, we were glaring at each other as if we hated each other. Suddenly she was not my sort; as Gordon Graham was not my sort. I mean, our family wasn't poor. My dad ran the biggest hardware shop in Garmouth. But these tennis-club lot, they lived on the seafront in Georgian houses that were so grand and old they had rising damp. Solicitors and doctors and maybe the odd accountant or bank manager, if he was lucky . . . they thought they were God's gift to the world, and regarded the holidaymakers on the beach as something akin to a plague of wasps. They actually wrote to the local paper every year to complain about them.

A remark of Fatty Alderson's came back to me . . .

'I'll push off now, then,' I said. 'Since I've fulfilled my purpose. All the top females practise against fellers. Fellers hit the ball harder. Thanks for making me your chopping-block . . .'

I turned away blindly, close to tears, though I think they were tears of rage and humiliation.

'Jimmy,' she said. 'Come back. It's not *like* that . . .'

But that was all I heard. Because the next second I had a very pleasant sensation. I'd blindly walked smack into Pat Hope. She fell on her back on the grass, and I fell on top of her. I put out my hands to save myself and stop me squashing her flat, and unwittingly grabbed hold of bits of Pat Hope that you weren't supposed to grab hold of. Not in public, in front of half the school, anyway . . .

Surprisingly she didn't seem to mind. She grinned up at me and said, 'Steady on, killer. Let's save that till later.'

I let go of her reluctantly, and helped her to her feet. Her smooth face was a wonderful pink; she had blushed to the roots of her blonde hair. And her bright blue eyes were laughing and wicked.

'Sorry,' I mumbled. 'I wasn't looking where I was going. I'm a bit upset.'

Her smile grew wickeder. 'I gather the Queen Bitch isn't inviting you to be her partner in the mixed doubles?'

'No,' I said miserably.

'Will you be *my* partner, Jimmy Tuffin?'

She'd been eavesdropping. It should have warned me. And the wicked glint in her eyes should have warned me too. I knew she was no friend of Felicity's. But neither was I, now. Stuff Felicity, and stuff her posh lawyer tennis-playing father. I'd bloody show them . . .

'Yes,' I said. 'With all my heart.'

'Garmouth Park, Monday morning, ten o'clock, tiger!' she said. 'We've got a lot of work to do.'

As we walked off to lessons at the sound of the bell, I looked back. Felicity still stood there, and I've never seen anyone look so lonely.

Tough!

I learned a lot in the next week. I learned a lot on court. Pat Hope had really watched other players playing, and she knew the weaknesses of each of them. Trudy Gray had a terrific forehand, but no backhand, so you always played to Trudy's backhand. Sonia Moreton had a wicked first serve, but her second was so soft and slow it was made to hit, so you stepped up to it, nearly to the service-line. Julia Berger wore specs, and had trouble smashing when she was looking into the sun. Pat Hope had a very sharp, wicked, little mind.

But if her mind was wicked, her body . . . I mean, it was a neat little body that could get around the court very fast. But she had such curves, and a creamy skin above the neck of her tennis-dress that seemed to *glow* . . . And on those quiet mornings, when the park-keeper was nowhere about, she used to call me into the girls' changing-room to discuss one more point . . . I just never realised a girl's skin could *feel* like Pat Hope's. Not that she let me go too far, but there was plenty of it. Enough to keep me more than happy. Enough to erase every memory of Felicity's slimness from my mind. Except one. That Felicity was the enemy now; Felicity was the monster.

And she told me plenty about Felicity's family. What snobs they were. How nobody was good enough for them. How they were always trying to get people they considered 'the wrong people' kept out of Garmouth Tennis Club.

And Gordon Graham . . . how she had seen Felicity in Gordon Graham's sports car just last night. Parked on the promenade at dusk. And they were cuddling and snogging.

I tried to stay cool, or act cool anyway. 'I expect she only wants to win the mixed doubles . . .'

'Oh, no,' said Pat. 'She was going to ask you to be her partner. But dear Daddy said you weren't the sort they wanted playing at

Garmouth Tennis club. Your strokes were like a baboon's, and you were only a shopkeeper's son . . .'

'Gordon Graham's only a shopkeeper's son.'

'Ah, but his father sells *diamonds*! Not lavatory brushes!'

'He said *that*?'

'He said that at the Club. On the verandah. Everybody laughed.'

I believed every word of it.

It ceased to be a tennis tournament. It became a crusade. I would show the bastards. I'd make them laugh on the other sides of their faces. The workers of Garmouth were on the march against the snobs, and I was leading it.

Pat Hope showed me a few sneaky tricks of her own on the tennis-court, as well.

My mum bought me two new pairs of white socks, and a new white tennis-shirt with 'Dunlop' on the left breast. Even though clothes were still on ration.

My dad was a bit more dubious.

'Moving in exalted circles are we, lad?'

'I suppose so.'

'Be careful . . .'

'I can play as well as they can.'

'I wasn't talking about the tennis. That kind of place, more goes on on the verandah and in the changing-rooms than on the court . . . people can be very cruel, if they think you're not their sort. I've had some in the Masons . . .'

So you see, even my wise dad was rooting for Pat Hope.

But he was right. Even before the first game had started, even before they knew how I could play, they were picking at me. They noticed that my tennis-shoes were starting to fray at the toe. They noticed the unusual twin buckles of my naval officer's white shorts. They noticed that my tennis-racket, that I'd bought second-hand, had rather an unusual broad head. Old-fashioned . . .

And they said so. Quietly, but just loudly enough so I could hear. And laughed . . . jollily.

I didn't make the *good* discovery till I started to play. The difference between grass and tarmac. On tarmac, my forehand bounced high and slow, and even my most viciously cut backhand rose a few inches off the surface.

On grass, my forehand went fast and low, and some of my backhands didn't lift off the grass at all.

And, of course, in those days, there were certain gentlemanly conventions. Like you, as a gentleman, did not use your hardest serve on ladies . . .

I did not play like a gentleman at all. The other pair never knew what had hit them. We won 6–2, 6–1, and walked off into a hating silence. No more laughter; just pure upper-middle-class loathing. I heard later our girl opponent was in tears in the changing-room. I heard that certain adults had tried to insist to the umpire that I was immediately banned from the tournament . . . Pat had certainly got very sharp ears, and kept them open.

Pat and I sat alone, in between matches. A conspiratorial huddle.

Saying as nasty things about them as they were saying about us. I watched Felicity win her first singles. It struck me she wasn't playing all that well. Her face was set and closed-up; she looked more queenly than ever. Though now, of course, she was the wicked queen. Then I watched her play doubles with Gordon Graham, after lunch. Graham was very flashy; but again Felicity was below her best, and made a lot of silly mistakes, including double-faults. And it struck me then that Gordon Graham and she didn't act towards each other like they were very close. They hardly spoke to each other, and at the end walked off in separate directions, after they'd won in three sets.

But I didn't have time to wonder about it, because then we were on that same court.

The opening game I served; and it was unfortunate. My first serve was always a bit erratic. Half the time it went into the net, with a terrifying bang that at least served to scare the females. But sometimes it went the other way, very long. On this occasion it hit the female in the chest. I didn't mean to do it, it just happened.

She had to leave the court to recover. The adults by this time were gathering in a group on the verandah that looked very like a lynch-mob. It was an uncomfortable ten minutes, just standing there, being glared at.

When she came back her nerve was gone. She just stood there shaking with her eyes shut, when I served her my first service. I mean, I even softened it down a bit, I'm not a thorough-going bastard. But it just sailed past her.

We won, 6–2, 6–3. Pat did a lot of sneaky work at the net.

We were in the quarter-finals.

Then the next day our next opponents scratched. Nobody gave any reason, but the looks I got were poison.

We were in the semi-finals.

Meanwhile, my little accomplice, Pat Hope, was doing very nicely in the ladies' singles. I mean, not that I didn't expect her to; she was on our tennis team as a regular, probably the next best to Felicity that we had. But it was the *way* she won. Because, surprise, surprise, she beat the very girls she had been talking to me about. She must have had foreknowledge of the tournament lists; who was down to play who. I hadn't even seen the lists till I turned up the first day; neither, to my knowledge, had anybody else. But our little Pat must have had her spies everywhere . . .

And the cunning of the girl. She was small; she didn't have big, heavy strokes; but she could place the ball anywhere she wanted, on to a sixpence laid on the court. And she was good at lobs and drop-shots, which a lot of kids aren't at that age. Most kids, even good kids, are content if the ball goes in court.

But Pat . . . the first day she played our school's number four, Trudy Gray, who had a big forehand and no backhand worth mentioning. Every reply of Pat's went into that backhand court. Trudy was reduced to running round her backhand, then almost to gibbering, lost 6–0, 6–1. It left a bit of a nasty taste in my mouth. It was cruel; what's more it was boring.

Then Sonia Moreton's second serve got thoroughly clobbered, and on top she began to double-fault, and the result wasn't much better. And poor Julia Berger, peering up through her specs into the sun . . .

In the semi-finals, Pat was up against a splendid big-hitting red-haired girl from Whitley Bay Grammar, a girl so good the whole school often gathered to watch her play, without being asked. Rita Mornington. Rita *was* splendid; until Pat started her display of spin. Top-spin, back-spin, sliced side-spin, and all so slow through the air. It went to four-all, first set, until poor Rita lost her temper at the torment and began hitting her drives out. It was like watching some splendid creature like a lioness or an eagle, caught in some devil's trap. Ugly. Boring.

But what the hell did I care? Our side was winning, and there were only two on our side, and all the rest of them on their side, and I didn't care how we won, as long as we won. So I cheered and clapped loudly when Pat made the finals, and my clapping and cheering was loud in the stony silence of the court.

Our wicked queen was making progress too; but slowly, painfully. Never in less than three sets, and she nearly lost her semi; had to save four match points, and by the time she had won she just stood with her head down, on the court for ages, as if she'd lost instead. I began to hear people muttering about *her*, as well. That she was past her best, that she'd peaked too early, that she was one of those precocious ones, who fade. Nobody really loves last year's champion, especially if she's been champion three times already . . .

Later that same day, though, she and Gordon Graham got into the semis of the mixed doubles too.

And guess who they were playing?

We all made it out to the umpire's chair at about the same time, and began fiddling with our gear, and giving each other those surreptitious glances.

'C'mon,' muttered Pat to me. 'What *are* her weaknesses? You've played with her often enough. You *promised* you'd tell me today!'

I shrugged. I might hate Felicity now, but I didn't have much taste for playing Judas. So I'd kept my mouth shut, to all Pat's little wheedlings, so far. But she went on wheedling.

'Hey, whose side are you on? 'Bout time you made up your mind, Sunny Jim! Or are you still carrying a torch for her, deep in your heart; after all she's done to you? Oh, the pangs of unrequited love . . .'

That stung me. I said, 'She hates balls that come straight at her.'

'*Ha.*' said Pat. It was an ugly sound. 'I hadn't spotted that. Girls don't go in for that, much.'

'Neither do boys. I just found out by accident . . .'

'Softie!'

'Will you begin knocking-up, please?' asked the adult umpire, in a very grand Wimbledon impersonation.

Knocking up, I never looked at Felicity at all; except one sorrowing glance of memory at her frilly knickers as she bent to pick up a ball. I was too busy exchanging glares with Gordon Graham, while we were having a little private contest to see who could knock each other's rackets out of each other's hands.

Gordon Graham won the spin, rough or smooth, and elected to serve. The first set went fairly quietly and we won it 6–4, mainly because Felicity seemed so weary, and Pat retrieved like hell on the base-line. I told myself I had a damned good little partner, and I was lucky to have her, even aside from the cuddles in the ladies' changing-rooms . . .

When we got up for the second set, Pat walked beside me all the way, her hand on my arm, as she whispered sweet nothings in my ear. She smelled very nice, but it was a bit embarrassing really, in front of all those people. As we parted, she bobbed up and gave me a tiny peck on the cheek, which was worse. And then she turned and laughed at somebody across the net.

It was Felicity, and from the frozen look on her face, she had seen everything. Pat gave her another nasty laugh.

It didn't do much for my game; in fact it made me curiously wobbly. But it certainly improved Felicity's. She really began to hit them, and we lost that set 6–2. There was a very satisfied murmur of appreciation from the crowd of forty or fifty spectators, that showed me which way the wind was blowing. Those two snotty little upstarts were about to get their comeuppance! Good riddance to bad rubbish!

That was when I began to play nasty. Oh, nothing anybody could complain about. Just plan B, which Pat had taught me. Muck around when you're serving. Keep your opponent waiting. Go through a real rigmarole of shrugging your shoulders, running on the spot, touching your nose with the ball four times before you actually serve. Even, sometimes, throw the ball in the air and don't hit it when it comes down . . .

But then the *next* serve, you hit straight away, and catch them napping.

. Four all, and the crowd starting to get hysterical in case true justice was not done. *Their* good shots received massive applause, well played, sir, oh, lovely tennis, come on, Felicity! Our good shots were received in silence, or to the sound of sucked-in air through teeth clenched in exasperation. It's bad enough when fifty people are doing it to you; God knows how they feel at Wimbledon, when they've got eighteen thousand people against them. Don't tell me the English middle class has any sense of fair play.

That was when I began hitting the ball with all my strength straight at Gordon Graham, every time. He kept hovering round the net with that hideous waiting grin on his face, and my third volley hit him straight in the chest at point-blank range. He fell down, and lay there rubbing his chest and groaning.

'Oh, I *say*!' trumpeted an adult voice from among the spectators.

'Bad form. Jolly bad form.'

'We shall really have to vet the lists for next year . . .'

We were five-four now.

So then old Gordon Graham starts the same nasty tricks. And his first serve, the big one, hits me on the nose. Without bouncing. While I'm still blinking and trying to stay upright, I feel this warm stuff trickling down into my mouth with a salty taste, and then down my chin, and I look down and my brand-new Dunlop shirt is all splattered with blood. I mean, three more great gouts fall as I watch. The crowd give gasps of gratified glee.

'Serve the young pup right. Hoist with his own petard!'

I am led away by harsh, unsympathetic hands. First-aid? It felt more like being arrested. In the changing-room my head is cruelly forced down between my knees, which any fool knows is the cure for *faintness* and only makes nose-bleeds worse.

In the end, it stopped of its own accord; fortunately, I'm a quick healer.

Back I go upon court, a spectacle out of a horror movie. The blood isn't just on my shirt, it's on my shorts, my legs, even my shoes . . . my hands are slippery with it, and stick to my racket.

'You can't play like that,' says the umpire, in a disgusted voice. 'Go and change.'

'Into what? Going to lend me something? Or would you rather I played stark naked?'

'Don't be impertinent.' The crowd roars its approval. 'You'd better scratch and retire.'

'At one set all and five-four up?' I was truly incredulous.

They made a dreadful fuss; offered me a puny shirt I couldn't even get into, and that would have half-strangled me if I did. Then someone tossed a huge flapping shirt on the sacred turf, with a gesture of contempt. Well, actually it was a short white linen coat, with 'Carricks Caterers' in red on the breast pocket.

Purloined from the catering hirelings, no doubt. Still, buttoned up, it was loose enough to play in. Must have been a very fat caterer . . .

And we're fifteen-love down, with that shot that hit my nose . . .

We're forty-love down, before we manage to scrabble three points together.

Deuce.

Then, glory be, Gordon Graham double-faults. Somebody up there loves me!

'Van out,' says the umpire, as if it was being screwed out of him on the rack, like a Catholic's recantation of the Virgin Birth.

He's serving to Pat, and it's the big one . . .

Glory, it comes sailing back, past my ear. Well up, partner!

It's coming back hard from Gordon Graham, straight at me. And Felicity is at the net, only feet away. I'm cornered, and Felicity has never been known to miss a volley at the net. *We're* dead!

I hit it straight at her, with every ounce of hate in me.

Somehow she gets it back, a bit feebly.

I hit it straight at her again.

Again it comes back feebly.

The third time I hit it at her, I screamed, 'bitch!' I don't think anybody heard what I yelled. Except her. Her racket twisted in nerveless fingers and the ball flew high in the air and landed in the next court.

'Match to Mr Tuffin and Miss Hope,' grates out the umpire; he sounded like the speak-your-weight machine in Garmouth Park, which is always running down.

Next day was the finals. I wore my white rugby shorts, and my mum cut down an old white formal shirt of my father's to short sleeves. I had my other pair of socks, and four layers of whitening on the blood-stains on my shoes. Nobody spoke to me, except Pat.

She and Felicity were on first; the ladies' singles. Felicity walked on to court looking like death warmed up. What the hell *was* the matter with her? Had she fallen out with lover-boy Gordon Graham? He was sitting right next to the court, on the pavilion steps, and she didn't even look at him. He was chatting away to what passed for his mates. Stuck-up lot. He couldn't have cared less about her. He gave her one quick glance, as if she was someone who was getting in his light or something. It was a glance that said more than that he didn't care. It said he had *never* cared . . .

A faint suspicion clutched at my heart. I turned to Pat.

'Not now,' she said crossly, adjusting the lace of her right shoe. 'This is my big day. The day I've been waiting for all my life. I'm tired of playing second fiddle to that bitch.' She sounded so sure of herself, so smug, so self-satisfied. And suddenly so uninterested in me . . .

Who had told me that they'd seen Felicity snogging with Gordon Graham?

Pat. Only Pat.

Who had told me about Felicity's family and their revolting little habits?

Only Pat.

Who had come straight into the quarrel between Felicity and me, and broken us up?

Only dear Pat.

I remembered Felicity calling, that day we broke up.

'Jimmy. It's not *like* that . . .' The agonised look on her face. I might have gone back. We might have made it up.

But in stepped Pat.

I knew what was wrong with Felicity.

Felicity loved me. And because she loved me, Felicity was going to her doom, in the hands of this scheming female spider, spinning her webs. Who had used me. Who didn't give a damn for me either. All that kissing and cuddling on court. Aimed like a forehand at Felicity.

But what could I *do*? They were already knocking up, in front of two hundred spectators. She was as inaccessible as the mountains of the moon.

And then she mis-hit a ball. Over my head, fast.

But I caught it. I told you I had a quick eye. No slip-fielder for England could have done better.

Then she mis-hit another. I had to push Neil Pascoe out of the way to get to that one. People began to tut; that wretched Tuffin creature was at it again.

Then I got up and stepped out on to the court, with the two bright new balls in my hand. Like the ball-boys do at Wimbledon. Felicity looked at me, surprised, her face open and naked.

I bounced the first ball to her, from a couple of yards away.

'Sorry,' I said. 'Sorry. I love you!'

Then I bounced the second.

'*Murder* the scheming bitch,' I said. 'Best of British!'

The spectators were starting to murmur angrily at my presence on court. But I had got my message across. Her whole face broke into a smile of understanding. She straightened her shoulders and . . .

It was soon over. She was the queen again, secure on her throne. It only took forty minutes. Six-two, six-one.

Pat Hope didn't even wait to shake Felicity's hand. She left Felicity standing there at the net with her hand outstretched; flung herself with stamping feet across the court, her flaxen hair in its tight, tennis-player braids oddly white against the deep red of her face.

'Bastard,' she said to me, and flung her stuff into her bag and stamped out of the court, out of the club and out of my life for ever.

Felicity's farewell was a little more gracious. After she had received the tiny cup (curtsying gracefully to the chairman's wife), she lingered a moment on the steps of the pavilion where her family were sitting, and gave me such a long solemn look across the court. Such a look of sadness and regret, that she might have been standing a foot away from me. Then she raised her hand in a gesture that had a lot of goodbyes in it. And was gone, long-limbed, into the changing-room.

I never saw *her* again either. It was a long, hot, boring summer, before I went on to Durham University to study architecture. I thought a lot about her, those months, walking the walks we had once taken together. Maybe it was just too much for her, to have anything more to do with Scruff Tuffin, in the face of family opposition. Or maybe I'd hurt her more than she could ever risk again.

I never forgot her. But I remembered her most vividly during the eighties housing boom, when Garmouth Tennis Club fell on hard times and came up for sale. I rang a rich developer, Paul Edmunds, who was a mate of mine, and we came down to see it together. I persuaded him that with its view out over the piers, it would be an agreeable site for four-bedroomed detached executive houses. Of course, there was a howl from the middle classes, when it was too late and we'd got planning permission. I enjoyed that. Paul and I wandered round the place a last time, before the bulldozers moved in. It seemed a smaller, poorer place than I remembered. How could it ever have seemed like Wimbledon? The white paint was flaking off the damp little wooden huts, and the tin plates on the scoreboard rattled in the cold east wind.

Revenge is sweet, you say? It was more than revenge. It was an act of sanitation, getting rid of a place where you could only play tennis if your daddy was in the right kind of job, and knew the right kind of people. And to hell with your backhand! As we sank below America, Australia, Sweden, Germany, France, Bulgaria, Czechoslovakia, Russia, Japan and even little Israel in the tennis world, it seemed an act of sanitation indeed. I thought we've probably got a potential world champion, but he's probably a young unemployed West Indian in Toxteth, who wouldn't know what a tennis-racket looked like. Maybe one day that sort will come up on the school or public courts, with half his teeth knocked out, playing ten-a-side tennis.

But one court of Garmouth Tennis Club remains; it's now my back lawn. The spot where she stood that day like a queen come back to her throne, one hand, only one hand, raised a little in a modest gesture of triumph; for she was always a lady. She's never married, as I have. She's Professor of Public Health at Hong Kong University. Maybe she was just always too busy to get married.

Maybe she loved me, as I loved her.

The
Concert

My dad says, if you've got it, they'll come for it.

He's got it. He's the best brass band conductor for thirty miles around, and though he's nearly fifty, he can still get the old ladies crying with his cornet solos, especially 'The Old Rugged Cross'. The trouble is, he only likes the old tunes. When the younger lads in the band want to do stuff like the 'Cuban Rumba Medley' he just ups and walks out. He says the sight of all the lads in their red uniforms jumping up and down in rhythm is ridiculous. But they soon come round for him, cap in hand, when the competition season starts. Then we're back to the good old stuff like 'The Posthorn Gallop'.

Unfortunately, I've got it too. I don't mean the good head for figures that often keeps the firm of Stretch and Fiddel, accountants, on the rails in times of crisis. I don't even mean my skill with the tenor horn in Dad's band. Nobody notices that, except when I have to cross my legs to play the tenor horn. No, I mean my looks. I mean the fact that I can't go anywhere without the fellers trying to start something. Just chat, mainly, except for those wallies who try to get to know me by spilling coffee down my dress in the cafeteria at lunch-time, then mopping me down with their spotless white handkerchiefs.

I often wish I hadn't got it. Honestly, I envy those girls who're just pretty enough to catch a feller who'll appreciate them for their cooking or their sense of humour. I've tried everything; wearing old jeans and a floppy jumper and my big, moony, reading-spectacles. But it doesn't make a ha'porth of difference, except to those wallabies who think they have the right to whip off your glasses the moment you're introduced and tell you you have lovely eyes.

Honestly, at my lowest I have considered becoming a nun; except even black serge isn't proof against their beady little X-ray eyes.

Which is why Matthew Winstanley was the first bloke who'd turned me on for ages. It wasn't that he looks a bit like Timothy Dalton in *Living Daylights*. I hadn't seen the film then. No, it was that he never tried to get fresh. He came to our office as a trainee accountant; and Mr Stretch always gives me the job of looking after new trainees and making sure they don't bankrupt one of our clients with a sudden stroke of misplaced genius in their first five minutes.

New trainees come in two sorts. The females, who listen to what you tell them, even if they can be a bit snooty at first to me, a mere book-keeper. The females never make the same mistake twice, and swot like stink every weekend, and pass their exams first time. Then there are the males, who spend their weekends boozing and crashing their daddy's car, and fail every exam three times and only qualify at the age of thirty-five when they finally sober up, if at all. Mr Stretch says accountancy will be an all-female profession by 1999.

Anyway, Matthew was always painfully polite. Always called me Miss Johnston, whereas with the other yobs it was Ros by the second day. He never stared down my front when he was bending over my desk; never looked at me at all, except sometimes at my hands when I was showing him something in a schedule. I have quite nice hands. And he always wore those three-piece suits, with their dinky little waistcoats, with the bottom button undone. It made him challengingly inaccessible by comparison with the sort who usually have at least one shirt-button undone, displaying a gold chain or a black hairy paunch.

Anyway, I did my best to cultivate Matthew. By saving him from every booboo a trainee can commit, and smiling at him approvingly, and even discreetly crossing my legs.

He rewarded me by continuing to call me Miss Johnston and giving me a huge box of chocolates his first Christmas. At least he didn't actually *give* them to me; just left them on my desk while all the rest of us went out for our Christmas lunch-time booze-up. With a little card saying, 'Thanks for everything. Matthew C. Winstanley.'

Things got no better in the New Year. Worse. As he got more streetwise round the office, he came to my desk less and less for advice. He was learning fast; Mr Stretch said he was a credit to me. I could've wept. His only passion was his old Triumph TR7, more red and polished than my fingernails. I used to envy that car, thinking of Matthew polishing her on Sunday mornings, with that sensitive, compassionate look on his face. I sometimes kicked it in the carpark, on the way to my own Fiat Uno.

My one and only chance came when Prince Andrew got married. That July, romance was in the air. Romance and elegance. The National Trust at Seldon Park set up a day of festivities to celebrate the royal nuptials, including a concert by the ornamental lake in the evening. The Hallé Orchestra; playing Handel's *Water Music*, of course. Followed by Handel's *Firework Music*. Followed by fireworks over the lake.

It sounded like Matthew, somehow. Round the office he hummed the fugues of Johann Sebastian Bach under his breath. So I cut out the ad from our local paper, wrote Matthew a memo about our local club comedienne's VAT, and half-clipped the two together, as if by accident with the ad at the back. And dropped them into his in-tray, last thing at night. And said a heartfelt prayer before bed.

Next morning, Matthew comes drifting across in his latest pale-grey three-piece creation. 'Thanks for the memo. This ad yours?'

'Oh yes,' I said, inconsequentially. 'I've been looking for it everywhere. You know how paperclips are . . .'

He said yes, he knew how paperclips were. I thought he was leaving then. But he actually took a deep breath and plucked up courage to say, 'I didn't know you were musical.'

'Oh, yes,' I said, 'all my life. My father's given his life to music. We're a very musical family.' Thinking of all the hours I'd sweated over the marches of John Philip Sousa, and our Ernie who plays the tuba, and our Ken on the euphonium. 'Even our cat . . .'

That crack about the cat was a mistake. His nostrils quivered painfully, and I cursed my quick mouth. Then he said, 'The Hallé. Looks quite a good programme. You going?'

'I don't know,' I said. 'Most of my crowd is more into Duran Duran. That kind of concert's no fun on your own . . .'

'A summer evening,' he said, a bit dreamily. 'You ever been to Glyndebourne?'

I nearly made a funny crack about them not being a group I knew. But something told me to keep my mouth shut. So I just said, rather ruefully, 'No.'

He sort of drifted away then, and I thought I'd lost him. But as he moved round the office that day, his humming of Johann Sebastian grew slowly louder. And just before we closed, I found this memo on my desk. From Matthew C. Winstanley. Would I like to attend the nuptial celebrations at Seldon with him?

After much thought, I initialled the memo, 'Approved with thanks, RJ'. It seemed the safest way to reply.

He picked me up in his father's black limo. I wasn't sorry really, because sports cars can do terrible things to your hair. He was wearing evening dress, looking more like Timothy Dalton than ever. I only hoped it wouldn't get too dark while we were at Seldon; they let cows graze in the home park. Cows are not fussy and I didn't want him treading in anything wearing that gear . . . anyway, we parked and followed signs saying: 'To the Concert'. On the way, we came across two couples sitting on the grass round a picnic basket, right next to where cars were chugging up to the carpark. Getting the benefit of all the exhaust fumes and three cowpats less than a yard away, and drinking what looked like champagne.

'What're they doing?' I asked, amazed.

'That's what they do at Glyndebourne,' he said.

'Oh.' The couples kept on chatting vivaciously about Monteverdi's *Vespers*, whatever they were; they hadn't been arranged for brass band, or my dad would've told me. Perhaps the couples were high on a carbon monoxide jag.

I must admit the setting was beautiful. The sun was descending between red clouds, reflected in the ornamental lake, with the Palladian glories of the house at the far end, set in its park by Capability Brown. There was a sort of grassy natural amphitheatre, surrounded by great oaks, under which bales of straw had been set for people to sit on. On one, three ladies sat in evening dress. One called across: 'Matthew – my dear!'

I was introduced to three friends of his mother's. It was hard to keep my face straight, because there were about twenty of those spiders that let themselves down on long threads from trees hanging just above their heads. I mean, I went sort of cross-eyed, trying to smile nicely at the ladies, and keeping an eye on the descent of the spiders. In the end I couldn't bear it, so I said, 'Watch out, there's a spider just above your head.'

I knew instantly I'd said the wrong thing, because the lady said icily, 'Oh, really?' and raised one elegant hand above her, as if she was waving goodbye to the Queen Mum. The spider, crafty sod, retreated about a foot but you could tell he was just biding his time. There were things crawling out of the bale of straw, too . . .

I think I knew then all hope of romance was doomed. The chairs for the orchestra were set out by the lake's edge. Three of the music-stands had already been blown over by a steady breeze, which was driving gentle wavelets on to the shore. The turf had a soggy glint. I just hoped the Hallé were wearing wellies. Green wellies, of course . . .

There were about twenty music-stands.

'Not many in the band,' I said.

'Orchestra,' he corrected.

Perhaps the Hallé hadn't had enough green wellies to go round. But I just knew they hadn't sent enough people. As a band-master's daughter, I know what playing in the open air does. My dad's brass band, in a hall, sounds like Concorde taking off. Deafening. But in the open air, even with a bandstand roof to deflect the sound downwards, it'll only just manage to carry fifty yards.

'If we sit on these bales of straw,' I said, 'we won't hear a thing.'

'Are you sure?' he said. 'They know what they're doing, you know.'

Oh, you poor trusting child, I thought. You're one of Them, and you have to believe They know what They're doing. What about the Indian Mutiny, and the Crimea and the Somme? My father told me that a lot of good brass band players got needlessly killed on all three occasions. My dad's first rule is never to assume that They know what They're doing.

'I've listened to more open-air concerts,' I said, 'than you've had hot breakfasts. My dad's an open-air concert expert. If we sit on these bales, we won't hear a thing.'

'I'll get a rug for us, from the car,' he said, huffily.

I went down and sat on a dry tussock, just above the seepage waterline. Everybody else stared at me, like they expected me to make an announcement or something.

The band came on, stared at me as well, and squelched gently to their seats. You could tell they wished they had been wearing their green wellies. Matthew came back with the rug.

'We're so conspicuous,' he hissed. 'I feel like a fool.'

'We'll see who's the fool, once they start.'

They started. Handel's 'Water Music' was quite appropriate, in the circumstances. The players kept raising the odd foot and waggling it, like a cat in a wet yard.

We could hear them quite well; you just felt like turning up the volume a bit. I'd have wriggled my bottom a bit nearer, if it hadn't been for Matthew and the seepage; I like good playing.

Then the gentry up the slope, who couldn't hear a thing because the wind was blowing the music away in the direction of Ringway Airport, realised I hadn't been as green as I was cabbage-looking. A bunch of dowagers raised themselves from their horses' breakfasts and moved regally down the slope. In a second, the entire audience was on the move.

It felt like being on the receiving end of the Charge of the Light Brigade. Somebody hit Matthew on the head with a picnic basket, disarranging his hair. I saw him reach for his comb, before he realised he was In Public. Next second, somebody dropped a tartan rug over my head, plunging me into darkness. Then I felt the point of a shooting-stick descend between two of my fingers, and clutched my hands protectively to my bosom like Mimi in 'La Bohème'. Great shouts of, 'This way, Lydia, this way,' and 'Has Granny got the After Eights?'

I don't think George Frideric Handel would have liked it at all. But perhaps I misjudge him. At the first performance of his *Firework Music*, a lot of the crowd got badly singed by the fireworks, and the organiser went berserk with a sabre. The faces of the Hallé were now set in a look of grim determination, as the water seeped into their patent-leather pumps and they too realised it was going to be that sort of evening.

Still, dusk deepened romantically. Lights came on in the great hall, and reflected beautifully in the water.

Lights also came on in the beer tent, a hundred yards away up the hill. There'd been sheepdog trials earlier in the day; the tent was hung with ads for Tetley Bitter and sheep-dip. The sheep had gone home, but obviously the shepherds hadn't. Neither had the sheep-dogs; you could hear them barking. And now the shepherds wanted more light to drink by.

Somebody started a petrol generator. Concerto for strings and petrol generator. Old Prokofiev or Schoenberg would've loved it.

The shepherds obviously didn't. They wanted something brighter. Some kind of juke-box started belting out 'A whiter shade of pale', over what was left of the sheep-dog trial's tannoy system . . .

Grimfaced as the Guards at Dunkirk, the Hallé fiddled on.

As I have said before, dusk deepened over the lake. And dusk after a warm day, next to stagnant water, means only one thing. There was a sharp metallic ping, just above my head. Then the first mosquito bit me. And I in my best sleeveless mini-dress. Having shaved my legs that morning, I wasn't even wearing tights. It felt a bit like that scene in James Bond's *Dr No* where a man gets eaten alive by piranha fish. With a muted scream I grabbed the rug, sending Matthew sprawling. In a second, only my nose and eyes were exposed to the foe.

'You cold, or something?' hissed Matthew. I could tell he was still trying at that point to be understanding.

Without much success. Till the first mossie bit him, on the end of his engaging dead-straight nose.

'Oh, I say,' he said, wiping off mosquito and blood all mixed up, with his spotless white handkerchief.

I must say this for the dowagers: they did not lose their nerve and break ranks. They held as steady as the British squares at Waterloo. But, like those squares, they didn't take it lying down. They struck back at the foe. Souvenir programmes were waved and whacked in all directions. The Hallé conductor gave them a startled look, thinking they were joining him in conducting, as they do on the last night of the Proms. Then enlightenment struck, as the first mossie bit *him*. And so we finished the piece. Pom, pom, whack. Pom, pom, WHACK!

Rather scattered applause. The sort Ian Botham might get when he was out for forty, with England needing 200 to avoid the follow-on.

There followed a short break, during which the sound of the rejoicing shepherds up the hill exceeded Beethoven's version in his

Sixth Symphony. Some of the husbands among us, having been dragged along reluctantly by their wives, began to think refreshment might be a good idea, and began to make their way through us and up the hill. Not many people got trampled at this point, because although we were tightly packed, those in need of refreshment were both sober and unladen.

But halfway through the next piece, a rather sweet piece by Vivaldi, they began coming back from the beer tent with four pints apiece, two in each hand. Disaster was inevitable. There was a piercing cry, as of some exotic night-bird flying over the lake, as a buxom wench of thirty got two pints of lager straight down the back of her backless tulle creation.

Vivaldi's concerto for strings and male voices (threatening to horse-whip on one side, and knock teeth down throats on the other).

And then the direction of the wind changed. It blew cold from the west; it blew away the midges and mosquitos; it blew away the sound of Elton John from the beer tent.

And it changed the landing-pattern into Ringway Airport.

And I saw a sight that made the whole night worthwhile; a sight I shall never forget as long as I live.

A 747 coming down into Ringway at five hundred feet, flaps down, stately as a galleon, gilded by the last rays of the setting sun. To the opening bars of Handel's *Firework Music*. And the sight and the music fitted perfectly.

I actually heard the music, as the 747 hung over the ornamental lake, because the awful noise a jet makes doesn't hit you till it is past. And then the equally amazing sight of the Hallé fiddling frantically, ten yards away, and you couldn't hear a single note.

That was when the conductor flung his baton in the water; and then had to go on conducting without it. Not that it mattered much, because suddenly it was rush-hour at Ringway. They were coming in from the Costa Brava at one a minute. I said to Matthew I thought it was a unique audio-visual experience.

He did not seem inclined to agree.

We did not stay till the end. By this time, the carriers of drinks were so tipsy, they might as well have thrown all four pints straight into the crowd as soon as they reached it.

I saw a fat man approaching with three pints in each hand.

It was too much for Matthew. He leaped to his feet with both arms upraised. He looked oddly heroic, like some Victorian signalman stopping the express train before it crashed over the collapsed bridge.

'Not another foot!' he cried. 'Not another inch!'

A change came over the fat man. He put his six pints carefully down on the grass, without spilling a drop. When he straightened up, he looked less like a drunk fat man than a half-drunk all-in wrestler.

'What-did-you-say?' he asked Matthew, sticking his chin out. Matthew looked ever so frail against him. But he said bravely, 'Not another inch!'

The all-in wrestler came in like my imaginary Victorian express train, fists flailing like a windmill. I closed my eyes in horror. There was a loud thud. I half-opened one eye, fearfully.

The all-in wrestler lay flat on his back. Matthew stood there, breathing a little heavily, nostrils flared, looking more like Timothy Dalton than ever. I was filled with pride. Matthew was the man for me.

My dad would approve, too.

And then, two men actually had the nerve to come over and say that they were the stewards whose job was to keep order, and they had to ask Matthew to leave. I could tell Matthew took that very hard; but he suffered in silence like a gentleman.

We went back to the car. It was hopelessly hemmed in by other cars. We couldn't move an inch.

It started to rain, just as they started the fireworks, an hour late. Soon we were sitting in the car in the middle of an empty field, our only company one crushed picnic basket.

'I'll take you home,' said Matthew between gritted teeth. And I knew that once he had, he would never speak to me again. Except to acknowledge my VAT memos. His pride had been too deeply hurt. In his own words, he had made a nonsense and I was the only witness.

All the way home he seethed and breathed deep, like a caged tiger. It was magnificent. And all the time I tried to think of a way of salving his wounded pride. But all inspiration had left me.

Till we reached our garden gate.

It had stopped raining. And there, up the big oak tree in front of our house, was our maddening old cat. Twenty feet from the ground, and mewing piteously. She does it about twice a week. The first time she did it, she was a tiny kitten, and Mum called out the fire brigade. She let them get within a foot of her, then looked insulted and climbed down herself. But ever since, when she feels neglected, she tries it on again.

She was my last chance.

'Oh, my poor pussy!' I wailed. 'She can't get down. She'll fall and be killed.' I started to cry. After the evening I'd just spent, I had plenty of crying stored up handy.

I must say that, once again, Matthew was magnificent. He went up that tree, in his patent-leather pumps, in a style worthy of Tarzan. Even our cat was impressed. She waited for him to pick her up, which was more than she had for the fireman.

It was just a pity that halfway down Matthew caught the back of his coat on a jagged branch.

For a second, he just dangled there, helpless. Then there was a sound of long, slow tearing, and he was sort of lowered towards the ground by the ripping ends of his jacket. He fell the last six feet and started hopping around because he'd hurt his ankle.

Well, there was nothing for it but to ask him in to meet the family. I took it at a rush. Burst into the sitting-room and announced: 'Matthew rescued my poor pussy from the tree, and now he's torn his coat and sprained his ankle.'

'But . . .' said our Ernie, all poised to blow the gaff on my little schemes. But Dad leaped out of his chair to greet Matthew, and kicked the little beast into silence with a sharp tap on the shin. Quick on the uptake, my dad is.

'But,' said the little beast again. My mum grabbed him, and hustled him out to help her make a cup of tea. Mum and Dad always know what each other is thinking.

I followed them out, to explain matters. They took a certain amount of explaining. Too much. By the time I'd got back, Dad had the big cupboard open, and all the spare brass band instruments out. Goodbye, Johann Sebastian and Vivaldi. Hello, 'Anchors Aweigh'. Goodbye Matthew.

But wait. Dad was offering Matthew his own cornet, a thing unknown in the history of our family.

And Matthew was taking it, tentatively, saying, 'I haven't played for years. Since the army cadet band at school.'

'Go on,' said Dad encouragingly. 'It's like riding a bike. Once you've done it, you never forget. You've got the fingers for it.'

Matthew raised the cornet to his lips, and after a couple of false starts, out came the 'Last Post'.

'Keep your head up,' said Dad softly. 'We don't want you risking a split lip.' He said it with a certain respect. Then, 'Do you know the 'Posthorn Gallop'?'

So it wasn't the 'Last Post' for Matthew and me.

But it won't be the 'Posthorn Gallop' either. I'm a cautious sort of girl.

When I can finally get him away from band practice after next month's competition.

But I can afford to wait. As Dad says, if you've got it, they'll come for it.

The Women's Hour

I think I was a pretty child; though I have never been pretty since. My photographs show solemn dark eyes, silky black hair, a smooth skin. Perhaps that was why they always wanted to kiss me.

Or perhaps women kissed more then. Nothing sexy about it; just great big hugs and smacking kisses, for nearly everybody. And the little fishing harbour where I lived as a child seemed full of women. Aunties and honorary aunties, friends of my mother. For a long time I couldn't tell the difference. Big-bodied warm women, in faded floral pinnies. Aunt Rosie, Aunt Nellie, Aunt Bessie, Aunt Maggie, Aunt Laura, who picked me up like I was a parcel and kissed me without as much as a by-your-leave. The sea of aunties stretched away to the expanding fringes of my world. Once, aged four, I ventured far too far and got lost. I was whipped up the moment I started to cry by a totally strange aunty, who not only kissed me but took me home, gave me first sweets and then drinks and, once she could get a word of sense out of me, carried me all the way home to my mother, who embraced her in turn.

Every street was safe, because it had an aunty in it, cleaning her windows or polishing her already gleaming knocker.

Even the men kissed me. I liked this less. Men had harder hands, they smelled of tobacco or worse, beer, and their faces had the consistency of sandpaper. Worst was my grandfather, who had a Kaiser Bill moustache that felt like a scrubbing-brush. How utterly *unnatural*, to have a scrubbing-brush forever attached to your face. Actually, my grandfather was the first casualty, the first I dared show reluctance about. I suppose I sensed a reluctance in him too. There was a stiff darkness in my grandfather; he had spent four years in the trenches, and drank too much to forget. Anyway, we were soon subjected to a shared female blackmail.

'Haven't you got a kiss for your poor old granda?'

'Give the bairn a kiss, Bob, it's not natural . . .'

My father was the next to get rejected. Coming straight from the engine-room of a trawler, he smelled of coal, soot, oil and other unromantic things. His sooty cheek *tasted* of oil, too.

But unlike the men, the women would not be put off by my unwillingness. They made their demands, and waited confidently till they were met. Even the old ladies with warts on their faces, from which grey hairs straggled. Agony, to be performed with my eyes tight shut, under the scrutiny of a dozen pairs of female eyes. I often worried that I was unnatural. I mean, I used to hear of other children who liked nothing better than going to bed with their grandfather for a nap every afternoon . . .

The only person I could bear to be cuddled by for long was my mother, and if she held me too tight, I would push away, shouting, 'Don't struggle me, don't struggle me.'

The termly nit inspections at school, when the district nurse, Nitty Norah, grabbed you by the ears and buried your face chokingly into her enormous bosom came near to putting me off women for life.

Relief seemed to come with the war, when I was nine. Suddenly I became as busy and military as a soldier. Even for the aunts, big cuddles turned into swift pecks on the cheeks. Mind you, I noticed that the general level of kissing didn't go down much, if at all. Our little railway station, on a Friday night, with the men coming home on leave . . . but this was sexy kissing for the first time in public. Couples running at each other from hundreds of yards away, as the trains came in. Flinging themselves, burying themselves into each other, while the man's kitbags fell off his shoulders and rolled about the platform, even on to the railway lines. And the girls had this trick of throwing one stocking-clad leg into the air behind them to show the extent of their love. One respectable married woman, whose husband was soon to go into the RAF, took to kissing him passionately on the doorstep every morning before work. This, the other mothers did not approve of. Best kept for the bedroom, our mothers muttered, and nearly ostracised her as if she was some sort of tart . . .

But there was no stopping it, even in the bosom of the family. When my cousin Charlie came home on leave, he and his fiancée took up permanent residence on the couch, coiled in a heap, muttering and giggling and kissing even when the whole family was sat there, and not a word of sense could anyone get out of them. I couldn't bear to look.

And in the fields . . . I became most reluctant to go up to the farm for a gill of milk after dark. When I joined the Boy Scouts in 1942, nobody said that bit about Scouts being clean in thought, word and deed more fervently than me.

But soon after that, a weariness seemed to descend on our harbour, and mostly among the women. I mean, my father was *spectacularly* tired. Life had always been hard for the trawlermen. They'd always had to snatch sleep when they could, with shooting the nets in the middle of the night, and getting wet through three or four times a trip and not eating properly. But now they had worse things to contend with; deadly magnetic mines dragged up in their nets, and Junkers bombers machine-gunning them in broad daylight, and them with only a single Lewis gun to defend themselves. Often my dad came home too tired to even eat. Just stretched out and was snoring on our sofa, in all his dirty gear.

So I hardly noticed how tired my mam was getting. She was always very pale now. And often she sat my father and me down to a good fried meal, but said she didn't feel hungry, would only have a little brown bread and butter. Looking back I realise she was half-starving herself to feed us. She seemed to have no energy. And all the women looked the same: old headscarves and backs bent over shopping bags.

D-Day seemed to put more life back into the men, in a bitter way. They talked about the end now, and Jerry getting what he deserved, and what they would like to do with Hitler. But I found my mother crying when I got home after school on D-Day, cock-a-hoop and avid for the six o'clock news. I told her she was being stupid, it was a *marvellous* day. But she said she was crying for all the mothers' sons who were dying . . .

It came home two weeks later. The girl who lived next door to us had a telegram. Her husband had been shot down and killed in the RAF; an air-gunner he was. They'd been married just two months; we'd all gone to the wedding, and they'd been so happy and so much in love. She was only eighteen, and we'd kept an eye on her, because she had no family of her own. She was often round our house for a meal. She was a pretty, curvy, blonde little thing, so full of life and so proud of her husband.

My mother spent two days round there, with her. We hardly saw her. And other women kept going in and out of the house all the time, with little wartime titbits, to tempt her to eat. But my mam said she wouldn't touch a thing; only drink glasses of water.

I kept well out of the way; scurried past her door in case she came out. I couldn't bear it. So when my mam said, about a month later, 'Why don't you drop in to see Margie? It'd be a bit of company for her. A bit of young life. She must get tired of all us old crows flapping round her,' I got into a total panic, and refused flat. And I would have gone on refusing flat, if I hadn't been in our garden, cleaning out my rabbits, when she came out into hers, to hang out a few poor bits of female washing. I was bent down behind the hutches, so she didn't see me. But I watched her, fascinated and horrified.

But she just looked the same old Margie. They'd said she'd lost a terrible lot of weight, with grieving. But she didn't look any thinner to me. Perhaps she'd started eating again by that time. Her hair was lank and greasy, and her frock had some splashes down the front, that was all. Her cat came home then, and she began talking to it, just like she always had. And I realised I'd been a total fool, scaring myself sick about her. Because I'd been a bit keen on Margie, in my fourteen-year-old way. I mean, just watching her when she came to our house, and showing her the best guns in my model army.

So I stood up, and said, 'Hello, Margie!'

She gave a jump and clutched at her throat, and said, 'Oh, Ben! You didn't half give me a fright jumping up like that. Like a jack-in-the-box.' And we both laughed a bit, and she said, 'It must be hot work doing out them rabbits. Would you like a glass of lemonade?' And I was so keen to make it up to her, that I climbed over her fence without going round to the front gate, and tore the crotch of my trousers a bit, but I hoped she wouldn't notice.

We sat in her little parlour, with the big photo of her husband in his RAF uniform watching us, all Brylcreem and sadness, from the sideboard. My eyes would not stay away from it, as I sipped my lemonade; it had me transfixed, like a stoat does to a rabbit.

She saw me looking, and she said, 'It's a funny old life, Ben. Some of the girls I went to school with are still in the sixth form. I'd have been there myself, mebbe, if I hadn't met Tom and got married. And now I'm an old widow-woman.'

She cried a bit then, but very quietly, just the tears running down her face and nose and chin, and splashing into the lap of her old frock. She said suddenly, frightened, 'Oh, I am stupid. I'm scaring you away. Sorry. *Sorry.*'

But I said, quite firmly, 'You won't scare *me* away.' And reached out and took her hand off her lap, and held it, till she'd stopped crying.

Then she said, again, 'Sorry,' and dried her eyes on a rather dirty hanky, and said, 'Tell me all the village gossip. I've hardly been out of doors.'

So I prattled on, about harmless things, like old Billie Toshack, the air-raid warden, who still went round shouting, 'Put that light out,' though there hadn't been an air-raid for two years. And the whale meat we'd been having, that tasted of fish till you soaked it for twenty-four hours in vinegar, after which it just tasted like vinegar. And that joke about Vera Lynn singing her song, 'Whale Meat Again'. I had her laughing in the end.

Then she said, 'Would you like me to cook you some chips?' though it was only three in the afternoon, and I said, 'Yeah, please.'

After that, I called in about three times a week, and I hope I did her some good. It wasn't hard work. She would cry a bit most times, but softly, and I just held her hand till she stopped, and it was nice.

Well, winter passed, a hard, hungry, weary winter. And then it was spring. And I noticed a change in the women. I mean, all the men could talk about was the advance on the Rhine, and the Americans hammering the Japs in the Pacific. But the women seemed to have a new spring in their step. I began to hear the word 'celebrations'. Mrs Pym, the vicar's wife, got the Mothers' Union to root in the church hall, under the stage, and they discovered, covered with dust, all the stuff from the 1936 Coronation Tea, which we'd held on the village green, at the top end by the church, on the cliff above the harbour. One

Monday morning, every washing-line seemed to carry a large Union Jack and endless yards of bunting. And Miss Martineau, the schoolmistress, began to rehearse mysterious dancing and pageants about St George.

My mam seemed more concerned about how you could make decent sandwiches with national wholemeal bread, which just crumbled when you tried to slice it. And there was a lot of coaxing of grocers, and bags of flour began to build up in our larder, and there were trips to the farms to coax eggs out of the farmers' wives. Everywhere you looked, there were women plotting in little groups.

Of course, people think now that Mr Churchill just suddenly announced the end of the war, and the whole nation spontaneously went mad. But in reality, we could see it coming a mile off. In the newspapers, the maps of Germany were so full of the arrows of advancing armies there wasn't any room left for any Germans. Jeff Lott said he'd give more chance to a broken fishbox on our stormy rocks than he would to Hitler now. So when the announcement came, we were ready down to the last trestle-table and cup.

That day, I flung myself into things. Men were scarce. Half of them were away at the war, and most of what was left were kids and doddery old gaffers who couldn't lift a tea urn, though my granda, who was handy with his hands like my dad, was a great help putting up the hired loudspeakers and gramophone. And Billy Sims, he'd got a scratch band together for the dancing. Violin, squeezebox and piano. And an able seaman on leave turned up with a saxophone. He was the only one in the band under sixty. And all the kids in the neighbourhood lent an enthusiastic hand with the huge bonfire they were building. There were so many wooden things we didn't need any more, like the bunk beds from the air-raid shelters, and signs saying 'Warden's Post'.

But it was the women who were so amazing. Working non-stop, gassing non-stop, flinging their hair around loose, with all headscarves gone. Throwing back their heads and laughing, enjoying exposing their throats to the sun. They didn't walk, they *danced*. I've seen it since many times at weddings, that dancing female step, that wanting to touch everything, that excited laughter. Every time a woman gets married, it's as if all her friends, married and single, are getting married with her. Whereas the men stand extra-stolidly, and drink and mutter, or fiddle with their big cameras and video recorders, so solemn. Why don't men join in rejoicing? What were they *afraid* of? If they hadn't been afraid of Junkers bombers and Hitler . . .

I mean, when my mother learned that our little fleet was going out fishing as usual that night . . . there was a real row, I can tell you. My father muttered about making the most of a sea full of fish and empty of Jerries, but . . .

Well, the day passed. The schoolkids stumbled through their tribute to St George, with loud embarrassed shouting voices. The girls danced beautifully, the boys resentfully. 'God Save the King' seemed to alternate with 'The White Cliffs of Dover' all day. And then it was time for the younger kids, full to the gills with seven different recipes for artificial cream (one said to include hair oil), to be pushed off to bed or at least to be sick privately down the toilet.

It started again around dusk, round the bonfire on the cliff-top.

The fishing fleet had gone; my mother calling after my father, in a taunting voice, 'Spoilsport.' It was then, as the band struck up, that I realised how many women there were, and how few men. And what men there were were mostly old gaffers watching from chairs that had been brought out for them. All those still hale and hearty seemed to be in the band, or fiddling with the loudspeakers, or gone off to the pub. There were just three young soldiers in uniform.

But the women were not deterred, as the flames shot higher and higher, and darkness fell, and the band went into an eightsome reel. The three young soldiers, protesting half-heartedly, were snatched up. And then I, just turned fifteen, and not even realising till then that I was no longer safe in the realms of childhood, till my hand was grabbed by a hot female hand, was snatched up too. I mean, my big plan for the evening was to throw on the bonfire, for a laugh, a German incendiary bomb that I had treasured for nearly five years. But the bomb bounced out of my coat pocket, and was never seen again. It probably wouldn't have gone off anyway . . .

Oh, how we danced! The firelight flickering on female faces laughing as if joy would never end, as if the world was reborn. Bare female arms flung around with abandon, female bosoms heaving under pre-war frocks, worn to the thinness of tissue. I was flung from female to female; there was no jealousy that night, no competition, they were indeed a sisterhood. And the kissing. I have never, before or since, known such wild kissing. I think I must have kissed every woman in our village who had two legs to dance on.

'Can I borrow your lovely boy?'

'Here y'ar, love.' And I was in another set of warm, embracing female arms.

Flames streamed from the bonfire like great banners. Showers of sparks, like glowing flocks of birds, floated away over the dark of the harbour. The world of darkness and death was done away, the world they had followed their menfolk into so faithfully. Now, it was the women's hour, and anything wonderful might happen.

I noticed with some alarm, in a brief pause while the band got their breath back, that all three young soldiers had vanished . . . I was practically alone.

And then she came walking into the firelight, quite alone. Margie. Her hair washed and brushed and behind a ribbon, her dress new, or at least spotless and pretty. There was a little hush, a little pause that gave respect to death for the last time, and then the band struck up again, and she took me in her arms.

And we danced alone, while the women clapped and sang in time with the music. And death was done away. And finally, ribbon gone, hair flying, laughing, she danced me clean out of the circle and into the dark, and the last view I had of the female faces watching us, they were nodding and approving.

I will not tell you where we went, or what we did that night. It is a secret I shall carry to the grave. All I will say is that it did no harm to me, and no harm to her, though she did move down to Whitby soon afterwards, to marry a Whitby lad who was a very successful skipper. She is a grandmother now, God bless her.

Nobody ever mentioned that night to me. Not even my mother, let alone my father, when he came home from the fishing with a wonderful catch of fish. But I often think of it, how wonderful it was, the women's hour, and how swiftly it vanished into the hard uphill drag of austerity. I wonder whether, left to themselves, women would make the world quite different, given the chance. And even whether, back in the past, there were other women's hours, when bonfires blazed on every hilltop and headland, and women danced, and their men weren't so reluctant to join the dance with them. What a very different world that must have been.

Claudine

When I first saw Claudine, I thought she was ugly. And stupid. How was I to know she was just lost?

Yet I should have known. Our parish hall was full of lost children, sixty of them. Little bundles of misery with a brown label tied round their necks, giving name and address. Bundled up in their best coats, far too hot for the May sunshine. Carrying all they had in the world in tiny suitcases, or carrier-bags, or cardboard boxes done up with coarse string.

Few cried; it takes energy to cry. We didn't even notice the ones who were crying till we saw, close-to, the shine of tears on their cheeks. They didn't make a sound, just sat there in rows on every table-top and windowsill like little parcels, waiting to be collected.

We tried to be kind, to speak softly, to smile at each one. But we were hot and tired too. This was the third lot we'd had today. Evacuees from London. So easy to treat them as parcels, to forget the homes and fathers and mothers that had been torn away from them so swiftly.

My mother was wonderful, holding their hands, taking them to the lavatory. This was important, because they were so afraid they would sit silent till they wet themselves, if you weren't careful.

But few smiled back at her. Most just raised huge eyes, asking the fearful, silent questions: who are you? What are you going to do with me? Some did not even raise their eyes, but just stared into space.

If they were parcels, my father was the postman. The vicar of this parish. The man who dealt with those villagers who had come to collect themselves an evacuee, as you might collect a stray dog from the dog's home. Could you blame them for wanting the pretty ones and leaving the ugly ones, the ones who smelled or had greasy hair and running noses? Could you blame them for wanting the older girls who might help with the cooking and washing-up, the sturdy boys who might join in the farm-work? Even if it meant splitting up the tiny families who clung together? My father did not blame them, but he was strict with them, and a vicar could be strict in those days. He knew all the families, the mean families who only wanted a useful pair of hands; who might starve the children. The families where the husband came home drunk and beat his own children. And he knew the kind ones too, the women who were poor, but made up for it with warm hearts and many cuddles, who would take three or four, even of the ugly ones. I can see him now, dashing from group to group with his notebook in his hand, little and quick with combed-back Brylcreemed hair and sharp eyes behind his horn-rimmed spectacles.

And I was the clerk, sitting at my trestle-table till my bottom ached;

like the Recording Angel, writing down where they had come from and where they were going to. I must not make a single mistake, even if I was just fourteen, nearly fifteen. My father relied on me; and I loved him. I would have died rather than let him down. That feeling is not so common now. I often wonder if any still feel it.

In the end, they all went. Our gallant Boy Scouts and Wolf Cubs began to clear up the half-drunk mugs of milk, and sweep the crumbs and crushed pieces of cake off the floor. Doing their bit for the War Effort; every crumb swept up a poke in the eye for Adolf Hitler. And I smiled at my mother and father, sharing our weariness. And old Jack Hawkins came in to lock up the hall, and said had we heard the news on the radio, that the Germans were still sweeping across Belgium as if nothing on earth would stop them, and our brave boys were retreating just to straighten the defence-line, and the French 75mm guns were taking a terrible toll of the German tanks . . .

We smiled again, with our bitter new-found cynicism, and it was then that I saw the older girl sitting in the corner, with her head down. I thought, till then, she was an adult who had come with the children, in charge of some of them. But now she made no attempt to move. She had high-heeled black courtshoes, but no stockings. It was considered vulgar, even in those days of shortage, not to wear stockings; it was what tarts did. Her long raincoat was fashionable, but dirty. Her hair had been done up in a grown-up style, but was now escaping from its hairpins and falling over her face in greasy strands.

'Who is she?' asked my father, in a low voice.

'She's French,' said my mother. 'She doesn't seem to know much English. That's why I left her to the end . . . a refugee.'

I felt wary. I never spoke to girls in those days, not even English girls. Girls would suddenly burst into giggles without warning; or even slap your face if you made the wrong joke. They seemed to be constantly on the lookout for a chance to giggle or slap your face. They were like living land-mines. And though the French, as everyone was always saying, were our gallant allies, the French were odd. Their soldiers wore sky-blue uniforms, instead of sensible khaki. Their planes and guns and tanks were funny shapes, even funnier than the Germans'. They were far too interested in love and food and drink, even in wartime. And they had strange toilets, where you could not pull a chain.

My father went across to the girl, and gently tapped her on the shoulder. She looked up wearily, as if for the thousandth time, and reached into her handbag and produced an envelope and gave it to him. I don't think she even saw him; giving the envelope was just a habit, and her eyes stared at the beams of the ceiling.

My father shook out the contents of the envelope. A passport and some papers, official papers. My father said, 'She crossed the Channel on the Dover ferry four days ago. Since then she has been to Canterbury, London, Guildford, London again, and now here. They've been passing her round like a lost parcel . . . What has she had to eat? Where has she slept? The poor child is worn out. Nobody would take responsibility for her, because she was French . . .'

'But we don't speak French either!' said my mother.

'To hell with that,' said my father. 'She's a human being. She needs a bath, a meal, a bed. We'll worry about speaking French afterwards. Anyway, our Ronnie can speak French . . .'

He looked across at me, expecting miracles, even though I had given up French at school a year ago to take up shorthand and typing instead, because I wanted to be a journalist. My last mark in French had been seventeen per cent; I was the despair of the French teacher. But for my father, anything.

I plunged in and shook her hand, which was long and slim, with long nails, which I thought very wicked, especially as they were painted red, and the red had chipped.

'*Je suis Ronnie Cafferty,*' I said, after long thought. '*Voici mon père! Voici ma mère!*' I couldn't remember any more of the French I had learned at school, except '*La plume de ma tante est dans le jardin*' and that didn't seem very appropriate to the present event.

A faint ghost of a smile dawned on her pale lips. Even in her weariness she was laughing at me.

'*Je m'appelle Claudine Deschamps,*' she said, and then I remembered that was the right way to say it.

'Take her up to the vicarage, Ronnie. Give her the spare room. We won't be long clearing up here. Carry her suitcase for her. She looks all in.' Then my father and mother turned away into more discussion about tea-urns for the next day with old Jack Hawkins.

We were a long time getting to the vicarage. Her case seemed to weigh a ton, and she was so weary she tottered on high heels and almost fell several times. She kept having to grab for my arm. What made it worse was that several of my schoolmates were about, tearing up and down on their bikes, no doubt supervising the War Effort.

'Who's your lady-friend, Caffers?' shouted Alan Jones, who was my worst enemy, as she staggered into me and clutched my arm again.

'She's French,' I shouted. 'A refugee.'

'God, Caffers has picked up a French tart. Ooh la-la!'

'When you getting married, Caffers?'

'You don't *marry* French tarts, *do* you, Caffers?'

'Faff off!' I yelled.

That only made things worse. They nearly fell off their bikes laughing, and some of the things they said, I was glad she was French and couldn't understand.

Then, to cap it all, she bent down and took off her shoes and walked on in her bare feet.

'Ooh la-la!' Alan Jones shouted. 'Cabaret! Striptease! Better than Gypsy Rose Lee!'

'I'll kill you when I catch you!' I shouted.

'Go on, you won't have the strength. You don't know what French tarts are like!'

My face burned like a furnace. And the unfair thing was all the time I was blaming *her*.

After a million years, we turned in at the vicarage gate, and they left us alone. Our front door was open; we never locked it in those days. I didn't know where to put her. In the kitchen? In the sitting-room? She was leaning on my arm all the time now, and she was pretty heavy. Her eyes were blank, and her mouth hanging a bit open. Perhaps she was ill, really ill?

I suddenly thought that if she collapsed, we'd have to *carry* her upstairs. And that would be *embarrassing*. Best get her up to bed while she could still walk.

I'd never realised our stairs were so steep. Or the handle of the spare room so stiff. But I got her in there at last. A plain little room. Just a narrow bed, a chest of drawers with a bowl and ewer, and an embroidered picture saying GOD IS LOVE. It was where we put visiting curates, when there were other people staying and the house was full.

But her eyes opened wide, as if it was the Kingdom of Heaven.

'*C'est jolie*,' she said. '*Très jolie*.' And fell on to the bed and then fell onto her side, and pulled up her long legs and was instantly snoring. At least, I thought she was asleep. But then she might have fainted, like the women who came to early service without eating any breakfast.

I hovered, uncertain what to do. I'd never in all my life seen somebody fall asleep that fast. Maybe she was really ill. She smelled funny, foreign.

But as I watched, to make sure she was still breathing, a change came over her face. The stupid look faded; her cheeks grew rosy in sleep. She suddenly looked like a little kid, like my cousin Monica when she was asleep with her teddy bear. And she suddenly looked . . . beautiful. Except that her right hand kept groping as if it wanted to hold something. It fingered the edge of the turned-down sheet, the bottom corners of the pillows, but they didn't seem satisfactory. I felt a great pity for that hungry, groping hand. I desperately wanted to comfort it. It seemed so terrible that the hand should be hungry, still wandering about, when the rest of her was asleep.

In the end, I went to my own room and got my old teddy bear. Not that I'd touched him for years; but I hadn't the heart to get rid of him, so he just sat on top of a pile of books in one corner of my room, getting dustier and dustier. I got rid of the worst of the dust by banging him gently, and making a great cloud of dust motes that hung in the last rays of the setting sun, coming in through the window.

Then I went and offered the dusty bear to the hungry hand. The hand felt him; then closed tight round him. The bear would do.

I felt I had achieved something great. I felt . . . as if I suddenly *owned* her. I surveyed her slender, clutching hand; the stray lock of hair that moved across her rosy cheek with every breath she took; her long slim bare feet. Such joy was mine. The joy of a fish that closes its mouth on the bait.

The moment before it feels the pain of the fisherman's hook.

She came down for the nine o'clock news, washed and changed. She had put her hair up in some beautiful arrangement, and she wore no make-up. Anyone could see she was a lady, not a French tart. She ate the sandwiches my mother had made for her with a daintiness that could not conceal her hunger; she gathered the last crumbs together on her plate, and ate them from the end of her finger. And she stiffened every time the newsreader mentioned a French town. As if someone had stuck a pin into her body. '*Les Boches*,' she would mutter. '*Sales Boches*.' Though she definitely didn't have much English.

'Ask her where she's come from,' said my father.

'*Où est ton maison*?' I stumbled. Was it '*le maison*' or '*la maison*'?

A stream of French flooded from her, that I was instantly over-whelmed by. But my father thought he caught the word 'Passy' and also the word 'Paris'. Not hard, since her address was in her passport.

'*Où est ton père*?'

We caught the words '*soldat*' and '*armée blindé*' and '*char de combat*'. Her shoulders went back; her back straightened and her eyes shone, though with a hint of tears, I thought. She was obviously proud of her father; and very afraid for him.

'I think he's a soldier in the tank corps,' I told them.

'Ask about her mother!'

'*Où est ta mère*?' I blundered on. But all I got was a flood about '*mère*' and '*grandmère*' and '*bateau*' and 'Calais'.

I don't know how we're going to cope,' wailed my mother. 'I don't know anyone who speaks French. What about your French master at school, Ronnie?'

'He's just joined up,' I said.

'She'd better stay with us,' said my father. 'Better the devil you know! If we give her back to the bureaucrats, they'll probably shove her round till she starves to death. Ronnie can cope. Meanwhile, I'll write to the French embassy . . . God help them.'

Cope? How do you cope, fourteen hours a day, with someone who doesn't speak your language, and who's worried out of her mind for her father, her mother, her grandmother, her home, her dog and cat and most of all, her country? Somebody who can't understand what she hears, or what she sees? Somebody who can't help weeping with the very strangeness of it all, however hard she tries to sniff back the tears, and wipe her eyes when she thinks you're not looking at her?

Well, you cope because you have to. We spent hours teaching each other words like knife and fork, bus, toilet, garden, field, cow, horse . . . You let her play the old wind-up gramophone till the needles wear out and you haven't got any more and can't get any more because there's a war on and all the steel is going on munitions to beat the Nazis. You dig out your sister's old bicycle because your sister is in the ATS and doesn't need it any more, and you mend punctures in both the tyres. Then you take the French person out on it, and she nearly gets flattened by lorries ten times a journey, because she keeps worrying about her father and her mother and her country, and keeps riding on the right-hand side of the road instead of the left.

And you take her to your favourite places, and it just doesn't *work*. I mean, there's a stream flowing through a little wood near home, and the sun shines down in a little glade, and you can sit with your feet in the stream with the water running between your toes and you can watch the minnows nibbling at your toes and the sun on the ripples and pebbles and forget about the war . . . and the first English sentence she ever manages is, 'Why are we do this?'

And all the time the war is going so wrong, with the British and French armies being pressed back and back to the Channel ports, and the retreats going on and on, and you are being told our troops are in fine spirits till you could *scream*.

My last trump-card was the old aerodrome at Chancely. I used to have so much fun at that aerodrome before the War. It was just a big, flat, grass field, with one rusty metal shed, but rich blokes used to come there to fly their planes and you could hold their tool-bags while they fiddled with their engines, and fetch things for them, and if you helped enough, they might take you up in the back cockpit for a little spin, if nobody more important was available ... of course it was abandoned now. But there was the wreck of a Tiger Moth, and the stripped fuselage of a New Gull you could sit in the cockpit of and pretend you were a fighter ace. And locked in the hangar were the remains of a Gypsy Moth that might be coaxed, one day, to fly again. The hangar was locked with a big chain and padlock, but you could see it inside, if you peered closely through the grimy, oily, cobwebby window.

All this I showed her. She managed to ask if the Nazis had wrecked the two planes, and when I said no, she lost interest and started her damned brooding again, sitting on the grass with her knees up in front of her, and her arms tight round her knees, and her chin on her arms . . .

I walked off; I was sick of the brooding. I mean, if we were all going to be slaughtered by the Nazis anyway, why waste what time we had left while the sun shone?

It was then that I found the new stuff. Pits dug round the edge of the field, with a heaped wall of sandbags round each. Over one pit, somebody had raised an army tent, and when I cautiously looked inside, there was a table in the dim light, and on the table a telephone.

The army sort, with a little handle at the side that you whirl round and round.

Well, I went in. Wouldn't you? And I picked up the handset, like they did in the movies, and whirled the handle.

Then it *worked*. A voice came through and I was so scared, I nearly dropped the whole thing. A man's voice that said, 'Stutely Fighter Control.' I was so paralysed that I couldn't say anything. The voice said again, 'Stutely Fighter Control. Do you read me?'

Then after a silence, another voice said, 'It must be kids, mucking about.'

Then the first voice said again, 'Stop mucking about, whoever you are. You are interfering with Air Ministry property and harming the War Effort as well, and if you don't stop it, we'll send the RAF police to sort you out, good and proper. You wouldn't want to go to prison, would you?'

And I dropped the handset back as if it was red-hot, and went back to Claudine, and suggested that we get away quick. She shrugged, and we got on our bikes and went.

Part of our road home lay alongside the railway line that runs from Dover through Ashford and Headcorn. As I was cycling along it, with Claudine trailing limply behind, I heard a train starting to overtake us. What caught my attention was that it was overtaking us so slowly; trains normally do that section like a streak of lightning. I glanced sideways, as it came level, and saw it was full of soldiers, coming from the port of Dover.

As the slow speed of the train was odd, so was the behaviour of the soldiers. Normally they hung out of the carriage windows, waving to all and sundry, and whistling at any girl they passed, especially girls on bicycles who might be showing a bit more of their legs than usual. But these soldiers just sat, motionless, staring blankly at the passing countryside. And many were still wearing steel helmets, which normally soldiers never do, as they're so heavy. And these men looked . . . dirty.

Uneasy, somehow, I waved to them, trying to stir them into life. One or two waved feebly back, but they soon stopped. For some reason it worried me deeply.

And then came a carriage full of men in uniforms of a different colour. Sky-blue. None of them waved at all.

But suddenly, behind me, Claudine went berserk.

'*Français!*' she shouted. '*Français!*' Then she shook my shoulder, nearly knocking me off my bike. '*Où est la gare?*'

I nodded ahead, bewildered. Then she was off like a rocket, pedalling like a fiend. I had a rare job keeping up with her. We whizzed through the little village of Headcorn, and up the ramp to the station. The train of soldiers was still standing there; women were handing them sandwiches and mugs of tea and handfuls of cigarettes through the carriage windows. Claudine ran through them, knocking them left and right in her haste to find her Frenchmen.

I followed, apologising to the women, saying, 'Sorry. She's French,' as if that would explain everything.

I reached the French carriage just behind her. The French soldiers looked different from the British. The British had looked very weary,

73

but glad to be here. The French had that same lost look that the evacuee children in the village hall had had. Lost in a strange land . . .

Until Claudine began jabbering such a stream of French that would have swept the strongest dam away.

What a change came over the Frenchmen. They suddenly crowded to the windows, all jabbering away just as hard, falling over each other in their eagerness. They opened the carriage doors and flooded the platform with pale blue; very filthy, oily, pale blue. They embraced her and kissed her on both cheeks, one after the other. Some wept unashamedly, but most grinned as if it was Christmas. One or two even whirled her off her feet and carried her up and down the platform on their shoulders. The women who were giving out sandwiches had a hard time getting through, I can tell you. I couldn't make out a word of it, except them saying, '*jolie, très très jolie*', and '*comme Marianne*'.

And then the whistle blew, and the engine hooted, and all the Frenchmen bundled back on board, and waved frantically as the train drew out, cramming every window. And Claudine stood so upright on the platform alone, like a soldier, with her hand to her forehead in a stiff salute, until the train was just a speck.

Then she turned to me. Her face was blackened with their oily fingerprints, like a stoker's. Her dress was stained where she had been held in their oily embraces. But her eyes were huge and shining like stars, and at the same time full of tears.

'Dunkirk,' she said. 'From Dunkirk. But they will return. To fight the Boche.' It was the longest speech in English she had ever made.

'*Ton père*?' I asked. 'Had they seen him?'

She shook her head, and suddenly she wilted. Then she straightened up again. 'I shall await every train. It is my duty. *Pour la France*.'

I tried to argue with her, but I knew it was useless. I cycled home alone.

For a week, she lived on Headcorn station. I think the women must have fed her. They soon spotted how she cheered the Frenchmen up. And by now, in a blundering way, she could explain what the Frenchmen said; what they wanted. Where she slept, if she slept, I don't know. My mother kept on driving up there in our car, with a change of clothes for her, towel and soap. Only one thing she asked for; a piece of red, white and blue material. My father found a piece, rummaging among the bunting left over from the Coronation in 1936, when we had a celebration tea on the village green. Claudine twisted it into a sash, which she wore across her shoulder; somehow she made it look French red, white and blue, not English.

She did meet every train; even those that came through in the middle of the night. A few times I went up to see her; but I found it too painful. Her mounting excitement as a train became due was awful to behold; she could not sit still, but paced the platform like a caged tiger. Then, if the Dunkirk train contained only British, or if the train was not a soldiers' train at all, she would wilt like a flower, and have to sit down and rest. And if there were Frenchmen, they mauled her so, in their joy, and she gave them all, with shining face, and none of them knew how exhausted she was. Afterwards, she would fall asleep in a porter's trolley, still sitting upright.

And never a word about her father . . .

And then the wonderful thing happened for me. One afternoon, I was digging my father's flowerbeds up, so we could plant vegetables for the War Effort, when six planes flew overhead. I looked up with great interest at all planes in those days; we all did. And I knew they were Spitfires, from their oval wings. I stood leaning on my spade to watch them out of sight, feeling cheered and proud. And then I saw the sun flash on their wings, as they banked and turned and started to descend.

From the way they vanished behind the trees, one by one, I suddenly knew they were landing. And they could only be landing at the old aerodrome.

All thoughts of vegetables forgotten, I leaped on to my bike and cycled like the wind. And when I reached the aerodrome, there they were, lined up as neatly as guardsmen on parade, with the pilots in their flying-jackets gathered in a little group, smoking.

But there were more wonders. A row of khaki tents had sprouted like mushrooms; a flagpole had been raised, from which fluttered a yellow wind-sock, and the pale blue ensign of the RAF. There were several lorries, and a stained petrol-bowser, and crowds of ground-crew.

But it was the Spitfires that drew me. They looked like great sharks, with their pointed noses. I could see the little patches on their wings that covered the mouths of their eight machine guns. I shook with pride and joy and desire, creeping as close to them as I could, without crossing the fence that bounded the field.

The pilots took no notice of me. They were laughing and shouting at each other, and waving their arms to imitate the flight of planes. And they were at the very far end of the row of Spitfires.

Greatly daring, watching them carefully out of the corner of my eye, I crossed the fence. Tiptoed up to the first great plane. The shining red propellor-boss, the neat tyres on the wheels, their every tread outlined by the bright sun. The shine of the open cockpit-hood . . .

Then I heard a shout, and turned and saw one of the pilots running towards me. I thought he was angry, and turned to run. But he was too quick for me, and caught me.

'Sorry,' I gabbled. 'I just wanted to look . . .'

He was not angry. He grinned.

'Ronnie Cafferty! Little Ronnie Cafferty! Still crazy about aeroplanes, I see!'

I looked at him; he looked so strange in his flying-helmet, with the radio-leads dangling.

'Don't you remember me? You held my tool-bag enough, in the old days!' He pulled off his flying-helmet and said, 'Bunny Beaumont, you old idiot!' and raised his hand and ruffled my hair. And it was the same old Bunny who'd taken me for flips in his old Tiger Moth, before the War.

Now he dragged me towards his friends. 'Chaps, meet Ronnie Cafferty, the best holder of tool-bags in the business!'

And they made a great fuss of me, ruffling my hair, and giving me punches in the ribs, and asking me where the nearest pub was. They were all very young; they didn't look much older than I was.

At last I was able to gasp out, 'What are you doing here?'

'Just a practice, old son,' said Bunny. 'To see if we could turn this old aerodrome into an emergency fighter station. In case the Hun gets too keen on Manston, and makes things too hot for us there. He'll never notice a forgotten old hole like this.'

'How long are you staying?' I gasped, still lost in wonder.

'Only half a day, and then home to Manston for grub! Piece of cake! But we'll be back on Thursday. These beggars need more practice avoiding the cowpats while they're landing. Mucks up the tyres so. Drives the ground crews bananas. But we'll be here all day on Thursday, God willing, and we'll be bored out of our minds. We look to you, old lad, to lay on the dancing-girls. Or at least a decent spot of cricket. Got a bat and ball? And a map reference for where all the best beer is? That so, chaps?'

They all grinned and nodded.

'And,' said Bunny, 'if you're a good lad in all this, I might give you a flip in my new kite. Bit of a change from a Tiger Moth, eh?'

I waited and watched them take off, one by one. Waited till they had dwindled into dots on the horizon, heading for Manston. Even waited while the ground crew packed up their tents and lorries and drove away with a respectful wave.

Then I cycled home in a dream.

The trains from Dunkirk stopped coming through Headcorn on the seventh day. The miracle rescue of Dunkirk was complete, and, filthy and weary, Claudine came home. Still without news of her father.

But she was a different Claudine. Tired out though she was, she carried her shoulders back and her head high. She had been of use to 'La France'. She also seemed to have got a lot more English suddenly. Perhaps memories of old school-teaching had revived, because they were needed so much. She still spoke jolly odd English, but now she kept plugging away till she was understood. And she was as determined as me to push on the War Effort. She began going round with my mother in her car, helping with the evacuees. My mother said she worked very hard, and the children liked her.

To me she was different too. She called me her first little English teacher, and ruffled my hair when she passed my seat at table. I think she was grateful for the trouble I had taken over her, those first few awful days. She came for bike-rides in the evenings, quite willingly. And when I showed her my favourite places now, she understood, and enjoyed them. We went to my stream and dangled our bare feet in the brook, wriggling our toes and touching them, together under water, which had a funny feel that made her giggle, because the water was cold, even in summer, and our feet were half-numb. I kissed her twice by that stream and she let me, and ruffled my hair again afterwards, with a rueful teasing grin on her face. I say 'she let me' because I can see now she didn't take me seriously. She was more than two years older than me; seventeen. But I was taller than her (though she was tall for a girl). She wore no make-up, her arms grew brown with the sun, her face freckled, and as strangeness left her and happiness returned, I suppose she looked and seemed younger than she was.

Of course, by this time, I was secretly but madly in love with her. Because, as the French soldiers had said, she was beautiful, with her long straight nose that just tilted at the end, and her huge green eyes that tilted up at the outside tips, to echo the upward tilt of her lips. A beautiful French witch who stole my young heart quite away.

So, between the French witch, and the English wizard at the aerodrome, I was happier than I have ever been in my life.

I kept the aerodrome a secret from everybody. For one thing, I was cutting school to be with the pilots and take them to the pub and play cricket. With the Germans sitting in Calais and Boulogne, just across the Channel, it seemed far more important to keep our pilots happy than to do maths and geography. I don't know what my poor father would've said, but he never knew. And besides, I was jealous of other kids finding out that the fighters were there sometimes. The aerodrome was three miles from anywhere, and hardly anyone went there, except the farmhands who mowed the surrounding fields. And I wanted the pilots all to myself, especially Bunny Beaumont. To me, Bunny Beaumont was a god. They were all young gods, always laughing and making jokes, but Bunny was chief god. He had taken me up in his Spitfire.

Of course it was illegal. At Manston it would never have been allowed. But at this aerodrome, Bunny himself was in charge, and nobody was going to split on him.

And you can fly two in a Spitfire, if the pilot leaves off his parachute, and sits on his passenger's knee. It helped that Bunny was small, of course. He was smaller than me, with his hair thinning in front and the little moustache he worked so hard on, with so little success that it was one of the squadron jokes. They were always suggesting he put cow manure from the field on it. Little he was, nearly as small as a jockey. But a young god to me . . .

Anyway, on my knees he sat, and off we went, him swinging the Spit's high nose from side to side, so he could see where he was going, so that he almost made me airsick before we left the ground. I couldn't see a thing. But then the tailwheel came unstuck from the field, and the plane levelled, and I could see ahead, over Bunny's shoulder, the line of trees tearing straight at us. He gunned the engine till it roared like a waterfall of sound, and then we lifted with a surge that nearly betrayed my stomach again.

After that, it was quite wonderful and I didn't feel sick any more, even when the sky above turned into green fields, and, looking out of the side of the cockpit, I saw the shining sun nestling among clouds beneath my feet.

When we landed, he stopped the engine, and pushed back the cockpit cover, and we just sat. It was funny, in a way, having your hero the young god on your knee, when I hadn't even had a girl there yet. The engine began to make clicks as it cooled, the rooks were cawing in the trees, it was sunlit and peaceful and I felt able to ask the great question.

'Can you beat them, Bunny? The Luftwaffe? The Stukas?' I was mortally afraid of Stukas, having heard what they had done to our army at Dunkirk.

'Stukas?' He laughed. 'Flying dustcarts. Knock 'em down like flies if we catch 'em. Piece of cake. Only got one gun and as slow as the Isle of Wight ferry. Not worried about Stukas. It's the Me 109s we have to watch out for.' He turned and saw the worried look on my face. 'Don't you worry about Me 109s either. They're twenty miles an hour slower than this little kite, and they can't turn as fast. And if you push them too hard, their wings break off. And we've got armour behind us there, and a toughened glass windscreen in front.' He tapped it softly with his gloved hand. 'Piece of cake.'

As I said, I lived in a daze of happiness, with the Hun sitting just across the Channel. I look back now, an old man, and know that fortnight was the happiest of my life.

And then came the day that France surrendered. A bright fine day. We listened to the radio all day. They kept playing a tune called the 'Trumpet Voluntary', an old seventeenth century tune. Its harsh bitter tones put strength into you, between the terrible news bulletins. It made you feel strong and bitter and brave, even though your stomach fluttered at the same time.

'Ah, well,' said my father. 'We're alone now.'

I looked across the table at Claudine. Her head was down, her long hair, unbraided for once, hiding her face. But her hands were clenched into folds on the tablecloth. The folds of the cloth stretched in a great arrowhead right across the table, under the plates and dishes. The knuckles of her hands were whiter than the cloth. I had an awful feeling she was going to pull the cloth right off the table, and all the plates and dishes with it. She spoke with her head still down.

'You abandoned us,' she said. 'You left us to fight the Boches on our own. We would never have given up, if you had not left us alone.'

Nobody said a word. Then she rose and walked up to her room.

'Better go after her,' said my father. 'You understand her best.'

She was sitting on her bed, with an open penknife in her hand.

'God,' I said, 'you aren't going to cut your wrist or anything?'

Her lips twitched, but it wasn't any kind of smile. 'The knife is for the Boche,' she said, 'but it would not even kill a Boche rat . . . I must fight, I must fight. *I* will not surrender. But there is nothing to fight with . . .'

'Come downstairs and listen to Mr Churchill,' I said. 'It will make you fee' better.'

'What is Churchill to me? He would not give Daladier fighter planes when Daladier asked for them.'

But she came down just the same. It was the night Churchill said that the Battle of France was over, and the Battle of Britain was about to begin.

'What is this Battle of Britain?' she asked.

'It will be in the air,' I said. 'At first.'

'Oh, what can I do about such a thing?' Her shoulders drooped again.

I took a deep breath. I would have died for her at that moment.

Instead, I offered her my most precious thing, the secret I had told no one, not even my father.

'I know some fighter pilots. They sometimes fly from near here. They have Spitfires.'

She gazed at me with empty eyes.

'Bunny Beaumont might even give you a flight in his Spitfire. He took me . . .'

Light came into her eyes. 'Beaumont! It is a French name. He is a Frenchman.'

'Sorry, he's as English as I am.'

'*Merde*. It is a French name. We have a village called Beaumont-Hamel. He must come from there – or his family. In French the name means "beautiful mountain". I will talk to him.'

I didn't disillusion her. Anything to get that hopeless look off her face.

The next time the planes came, I took her. She dressed in her best, with her hair up in its most beautiful style, and her red, white and blue sash across her jumper. I had a hard time keeping up with her, and I was twenty yards behind when she dropped her bike on the grass, and ran across to the little group of smoking pilots.

They stopped talking, and watched her come. To them, she must have looked quite something. And RAF pilots had an eye for pretty girls.

'Squadron Leader Beaumont?' she asked.

Bunny pushed out a hand, smiling appreciatively. 'Honoured to make your acquaintance,' he said. I think he'd spotted she was foreign, and a real lady.

'You are not French?' she asked, puzzled.

''Fraid not, ma'am. But anything else I can do to oblige you . . .'

'But your name is French. It is a place in France . . .'

Bunny pushed back his officer's cap and scratched his head.

'Well, they do say we came across with William the Conqueror in 1066, but it's a very long time ago . . .'

'Then you are *really* French?'

'Anything to oblige a lady . . .' Then he looked across at me, gentle, baffled.

I told them the whole story. Gabbling so fast in my embarrassment I don't know if Claudine understood half what I said. But all the pilots were very interested. They were bored, and with her eyes shining like that, she was beautiful.

'Must do something about this, Bunny,' said Taffy Lloyd. 'Can't leave a lady with only a penknife to fight old Hitler with.'

Bunny frowned, and then seemed to come to a decision.

'Mademoiselle, we will fight in your name, and in the name of France . . .'

'Then why are you not fighting now?'

'Good bloody question,' said Taffy Lloyd. 'One I ask myself ten times a day. We're not even allowed to cross the coast and fly over the Channel. Bloody orders from the top brass . . .'

'Mademoiselle, the time will come,' said Bunny gently. 'Meanwhile, would you care to inspect your new squadron?' He led the way to his own aeroplane.

She noticed the two swastikas painted on the side of the fuselage, below the cockpit.

'You are an ace?' she asked.

'Knocked down a couple of Huns in France' said Bunny diffidently.

'In my name, and with the blessing of God, you will knock down many more!'

All the pilots cheered.

After that, she was filled with energy. She sought out a Roman Catholic church in the nearest town. Having gently told my father that his was not a proper church, and he was not a proper priest. It was there that she prayed for the pilots, and lit candles on the gaunt wrought-iron candelabra to keep the pilots safe. I picked up that habit of lighting candles from her, and have kept it all my life. She even persuaded the Catholic priest to come out to the aerodrome and bless the planes. The pilots shuffled uncomfortably, with their hands clasped awkwardly in front of their groins, but I think they liked it, really. Pilots in war are very superstitious.

She also made sure that when they came, they would have hot coffee and something to eat; somehow my mother and she arranged it between them. In all this, I followed her around like a little dog. For school had finished for the year by then.

But still the Germans did not come. Instead, she learned to play cricket with the pilots; who much appreciated the flash of her long, beautiful legs as she ran after the ball. They also took her to the pub with them. They took me too, of course; but I had to sit on the wall outside, while they sent me out a half-pint of cider. *She* went inside.

I protested to Bunny; told him she was only seventeen.

'She's a young woman, Ronnie. People grow up fast in a war. Anyway, she'll soon be eighteen. And she's good for morale. You wouldn't grudge the lads, would you?'

Of course, I said no. But I was jealous, hideously jealous. They were taking her off me; I was the child left outside. Laughing and flirting with the pilots, she had no time for me any more; except to fetch and carry for her. To her, I was a child too. I thought of ringing up the police and reporting her for under-age drinking. But I had not quite descended that low; even on the day I watched them through the pub window and saw Bunny holding her hand under the pub table.

It was obscene. She was only seventeen, and Bunny must be twenty-three or four, really old. He was going bald in front. For all I knew, he had a wife, though he had never mentioned one. He was a cradle-snatcher. But far from being disgusted at his age, her face was lit up as I have never seen it. And so was his.

It was so much worse because I loved them both. Bunny was still my god, even if he was growing feet of clay. And she was still my precious one, whom I had saved by giving her my most precious things. The very English words she was saying to him, I had taught her.

I did not know what to do with myself. I walked away up the road, wishing that I was dead. Till I heard a shout.

It was an airman from the field, one of the ground crew on a bicycle. His face was very red, and he was panting.

'Are they in the pub, Ronnie? There's something up. Something big! Yellow alert. Five-minute readiness. The Jerries are coming!'

There was such a scramble. Both Claudine and I, back at the field, helped them into their flying-kit, which made them look strange, like Martian monsters, great bears clad in fur and kapok. The ground crew were starting up the engines. Before they scrambled aboard, Claudine kissed each pilot for luck.

Then a short wait, while the pilots kept nervously revving-up their engines, till you could have gone mad with the noise. Then the telephone in the tent rang again, and a man ran out and fired a green flare into the air. It landed in the hedge, belching masses of grey smoke. It set the hedge on fire.

And then they were off, in pairs, bouncing across the rough field until they suddenly smoothed out in flight, and their wheels began to retract.

We listened until their engine noise was lost in the song of the birds.

A long, long wait. We did not know what to do with ourselves, except to walk across and cross the field. We were so pent-up we could not even bear to walk side by side. The ground crews twitched around, moving the petrol-bowser, checking their strange equipment, the long boxes full of shining belts of machine-gun cartridges. Then they sat down and tried to play cards, But at the least sound of an engine, their heads would swing up towards the south.

The engines were always car engines, moving along the main road in the distance . . .

And then there were engines that were not car engines, that got louder and louder. Tiny dots to the south. One . . . two . . . three. And then no more.

'*Mon Dieu*,' said Claudine, and crossed herself. 'Where are the others?' Her face was as pale as a marble tombstone. There wasn't anything left about killing the *sales Boches* now. She was terrified . . . for Bunny?

But we had not long to wait. There were now two tinier dots, behind the three large ones. And then, one by itself. They were all coming home.

The first Spitfire touched down and taxied up to us. There was a hole in its tailfin. Just one little hole, but we both spotted it. The next four seemed untouched, but none of them was Bunny. You could tell from the numbers and letters on the side.

Then Bunny swept across the field, and rolled his plane over high in the air, once, twice, three times . . .

'Three,' I shouted. 'I think he's shot down three!'

And then we were overwhelmed by a mass of pilots shouting, laughing and throwing their arms round Claudine, and giving her great smacking kisses.

'I got one for you, princess! A bloody Stuka, over Portland Bill. Hit him right up the arse at fifty yards, and he just blew up. Nearly singed my moustache off!'

'Two. I swear I got two of the sods. They're rubbish. Slow as Teddy's old motor car. I don't know what we were worried about.'

'Even old Taffy got one . . . like shooting fish in a barrel.'

They acted like men drunk, punching and slapping each other. Bunny kept on saying, 'Steady down, lads, steady down. The War's not won yet.' But even he could not keep still for a moment.

And behind them, the ground crews worked like fiends possessed, getting the aircraft ready to fly again. Silent, absorbed, frightening.

Then the telephone in the little tent rang again. And every man froze where he stood, and I suddenly saw fear on their faces . . .

But the only message was that the Huns had gone. The pilots were to return to Manston, and report their kills.

Each of them embraced Claudine again, before they left. For luck. She *was* their luck now. Bunny embraced her last; and it was different. It lasted much longer, and when they broke apart, there were tears in her eyes. And she stood waving till he was out of sight, a mere dot, though he could not have seen her. I knew that something had grown between them that was so big that I was no more than a pygmy, an ant.

I left her, and cycled home alone.

That was the last we saw of them for a long time. The time for practices was over; the time for cricket and drinks in the pub and giving flights to kids. They stuck to their home base, Manston, now.

All but Bunny. He drove over to see Claudine in his little Singer sports car, and they would go off alone together. They had eyes for no one but each other.

I raged at my father. Claudine was too young, only seventeen. He stood in place of her own father. He must put a stop to it!

My father took me and sat me down in his study, with a solemn face.

'Bunny wants to marry her, as soon as she's eighteen, in October. I am trying to contact her father through the International Red Cross to get his permission. Though I'm not getting very far.'

It was like having a spear driven through my chest. It was as if she had died. It was as if I had died.

'She's too young,' I said, at last.

'It is you who are too young,' he said. His voice was sympathetic, but stern. 'Your time will come.'

'What does age matter?' I said. 'Age doesn't affect what you feel for someone.'

'That's what I'm saying. Age doesn't affect the way she feels, either.'

'Life's not fair. If I'd been five years older, I could have shot down a lot more Jerries for her than Bunny Beaumont.'

'It's not a matter of shooting down Jerries, old lad.'

'It's not *fair*.'

'Life isn't fair,' said my father, and sighed.

One evening, Bunny turned up when nobody was expecting him. My father and mother had gone to an important ARP meeting at Canterbury, and taken Claudine with them. So there was only me to open the door. I put Bunny in the sitting-room, and then felt I had to sit with him.

'Got a whisky, old lad?' he said, in a strange, muffled voice. As if he was ashamed.

Contemptuously, I fetched him a small whisky from my father's precious store. All the more contemptuous because my father had hardly any left.

'Thanks,' he said, but his hand shook so much as he took the glass that he spilled half the whisky over his hand and the chair. 'Sorry. I'm a bit tired.'

I switched on the light, for it was starting to get dim in the room, though it was nothing like time for the blackout. I sat looking at him. The bald patch on the front of his head was bigger. His face was very white, and there seemed to be new small lines all over it. He looked older than my father. He looked nearly as old as my grandfather. I was sickened at the idea that anyone as beautiful and young as Claudine should marry an old drunkard like this. I really hated him. But I had to say something to him.

'How's Taffy?'

'Taffy?' He seemed to come out of a daze. 'Taffy who?'

'Taffy Lloyd.'

'Oh. Poor old Taffy bought it three weeks ago. A flamer, poor old sod. No chance to get out of the cockpit at all.'

'How's Russ, then? Russell Taylor?'

'Got the chop as well. About a week ago. And for Christ's sake don't go on asking. All the ones you knew are dead but me. And the kids that came after them . . . there's only me left of the old lot.'

The flesh below his left eye kept quivering. And he kept looking at his watch, every two minutes. You could see he was having to make himself sit still.

'Is there another whisky?'

Silently, I got it for him.

Then he said, head down, to no one in particular, 'We're all shot to hell. No matter how many we knock down, there's always more tomorrow. Manston's bombed flat – useless. The ground crew won't come out of the air-raid shelters any more . . . look, how long is Claudine going to be at that meeting? Where are they holding it?'

'They could be hours. And I don't know where it is.'

Both lies. But I didn't care. I just knew he was going to die, and then Claudine would come back to her senses. And I wouldn't have to think of this old drunk touching her face and body any more. And having wished him dead, I wanted rid of him.

He got up. 'I'll be off, then. You don't like me any more, do you, Ronnie? What the hell have I done to you?'

'Nothing,' I said. How could I ever have told him? I hated him more because he couldn't even guess what he'd done.

'Goodnight, old lad.'

I let him see himself out.

I felt a hand come down on the bedclothes, and shake my shoulder. I came out of a dream of Claudine laughing in the sunlight, and saw Claudine serious, in the dim light of dawn in my bedroom.

'Hurry up, Ronnie, get dressed. The planes have come back – Bunny's planes. I heard them, and I've just watched them land. You must help me. I must get coffee and sandwiches up there for them.'

I got up, grumbling. I'd thought I hated her now, nearly as much as I hated him, but when it came to it, I didn't. Love's a funny thing.

We had a terrible battle to load up the bicycles; but we rode off into the sunlight with my parents waving goodbye in their nightclothes.

'Be careful, now,' shouted my mother. She hadn't wanted me to go. Airfields got bombed; even little harmless airfields like ours.

Claudine looked so young that morning. As I followed her, she looked very young because she was wearing white ankle socks. As if she was still a schoolgirl; as if she might still fall in love with me.

The airfield was very different now. There were nine Spitfires, brand-new and shining with paint. Some had not even fired their guns yet, for there were no long soot trails beneath the wings. There were no less than three petrol-bowsers, and a lot more trucks, and a lot more men, and even three Bofors guns for airfield defence. There were sentries, who wouldn't let us through, until Bunny came over and sorted things out.

Sunday, 15th September was a day in my life like no other. I suppose my dear father ran his church services as usual, and prayed for victory just a little harder. I suppose my mother cooked and washed up as usual, with uneasy glances at the low hills that hid the airfield from her eyes.

But I was in a world apart. One look at the faces of Bunny's pilots told it all, as he introduced us. Six of them, the old hands, were weary to death, could hardly keep their eyes open. The other two, new boys, looked rested, but scared, and kept licking their lips. But they all smiled as Claudine handed them coffee. Young men will smile at smiling young women, even on the edge of the grave.

The telephone rang well before nine o'clock, and they were away in three lots of three, bouncing over the rough grass. We watched them climb, and even before they were finished climbing, the waves of German planes were on top of us. Never so many before. Neat patterns of fifty and a hundred heavy bombers, so neat and precise they might have been drawn on the sky with a ruler. And the tiny crosses of enemy fighters, flying far above them. All heading for London.

Then the sound of machine guns, like a distant boy running a stick along distant iron railings. Hundreds of boys running hundreds of sticks . . . little swirling breaks in the German formations, as our fighters went in like mad dogs among sheep. Many trails of smoke falling down the sky so slowly, so small we could not tell if they were German or British. And then the massed formations re-drew themselves with precision, and ground on inexorably towards London.

We cheered our heads off, as we saw nine of our planes coming back. All were safe!

Until the wheels of one collapsed on landing, leaving it sliding along the turf like a screeching plough, digging up great heaps of soil, with its propeller bent into horseshoes. The pilot was pulled out safe, with blood streaming down his face. And one plane would never fly again.

Another pilot, having landed his plane, was carried off on a stretcher to hospital.

Seven took off, when the telephone rang again. Then the Germans were returning from London.

They did not look so neat now. They flew at all heights, some so low we could see their pilot's heads, and the numbers on their sides. We saw smoking engines and stopped propellers, and one bomber that had no nose left, and slipped and yawed like a landed fish, and we watched as it crashed on a hill nearer the coast, and cruelly we cheered the distant explosion as its crew died in a tiny puff of smoke.

Five of our fighters came back that time. Bunny came across to our dugout for a coffee, while his ground crew sweated half-naked to refill his petrol-tanks and re-arm his guns.

'Charlie Hill bailed out,' he said, talking to the empty air between our heads, a man far away. 'But Billy didn't have a chance; he hit a Jerry head-on.'

And the ground crews were having trouble with one of the remaining fighters. Its engine kept coughing and sending out great clouds of black smoke.

Four took off, when the phone went after lunch. Nobody was smiling now, not even Claudine could manage it.

That afternoon, there seemed twice as many Germans. They stretched as far as the eye could see.

'*Mon Dieu*,' whispered Claudine, pressing close to me without even knowing she was doing so. 'It is the end of the world!'

Again the flurries high in the sky; the vapour trails on the blue, crossing each other out, the slowly falling flamers. They meant little to us now, whether they were British or German. Again, the Germans passed over towards London. And over the low hills to the north, low clouds of dark blue that were not clouds. London was burning.

Two of ours came back. One was Bunny. Halfway across the field to us, he bent down and was sick. We ran to him. Claudine embraced him, in front of all those who were watching.

'It is enough. You have done *enough*!' In spite of all her control, terror was in her voice.

'Must get some more *sales Boches* for you, princess!' He took hold of her chin, and lifted her face from where it was pressed into his shoulder. 'Chin up!' He gave a weak grin. 'I think I got three Boches for you.'

'I do not want Boches,' she said. 'I want *you*.' Then he turned on his heel and walked away, and went and sat in his cockpit and remained there.

The other fighter was no longer fit to fly. Its gun controls had been severed by enemy bullets.

When the telephone went for the last time, Bunny flew off alone.

We saw few Germans returning. They say they took a route further east, a quicker route to the coast.

But we saw this one fighter coming. The sound of its engine was rough and strange; it kept on coughing and failing, and then starting up again. It flew with one wing lower than the other, and there was a long white plume of glycol smoke, trailing from its engine.

'*C'est* Bunny,' whispered Claudine, clutching me. '*C'est* Bunny.'

'He's damaged,' shouted somebody. 'He can only get one landing-wheel down.'

We were watching so close, with bated breath, that we never heard the Germans coming. We only heard our own Bofors guns opening fire, like a man slowly hammering on a wooden plank. They were fighter bombers, coming in low from the north. I don't know how they had at last discovered our little airfield; maybe it was the three wrecked planes on the runway.

But they blew those three planes apart, in a hail of bullets. One of the petrol-bowsers exploded with a blinding flash and roar; then another, and another. Ground crews were running for their slit-trenches in all directions.

I grabbed at Claudine. 'Get down, get down!'

But she clung to the sandbags and would not get down. 'Bunny. Bunny.'

And in his plane came, amidst the bursting bombs and bullets that tore the turf into fountains. He kept it upright, even on one wheel. Then it pitched down on one wing, and began to spin in cartwheels across the grass towards us. I watched it fall apart like a daddy-long-legs caught in a lampshade. The propellor blades bent up, the tail fell off. Then it stopped a hundred yards away. I saw quite clearly Bunny push back the cockpit canopy.

And then he just sat there, grinning like a fool. He made no attempt to move.

And then I saw an evil lick of yellow flame, under the engine.

He was going to burn before our very eyes!

I heard the roar, as the German fighters came in again.

And then Claudine was out of my arms, and out of the slit-trench, and running towards that plane. I saw her long legs running, her white ankle socks, against the pall of black smoke belching from the burning petrol-bowsers. Running through the hail of German fire, towards a plane that was going to blow up at any second.

My Claudine! I would not have run for Bunny Beaumont, but my Claudine was different.

I overtook her as we reached the plane; as another evil flare of yellow flame licked from under it.

I was on the crumpling wing, which crushed under my feet. I grabbed the stupid, grinning Bunny under the armpits. Thank God he had pushed his cockpit canopy back. Thank God he had undone his safety harness. Thank God he was little, smaller than Claudine, smaller than me. I felt a surge of triumph as he lifted in my hands. I felt another, as I threw him across my shoulder, as if he was a child.

'Run!' I screamed at Claudine, and then I was running, harder than I was ever to run in my life again.

The Spitfire blew up, and knocked me on my face.

I saw Claudine lying in front of me, with her lovely hair on fire.

Then she raised her hands, and beat the fire out. And all three of us crawled into a heap, as the German planes came in for the last time, and the turf boiled around us, and truck after truck blew up, and even the old rusty shed where lay the Gypsy Moth that would never now fly again.

Total ruin. Our airfield was gone. In one day, never to return.

But we three were alive, laughing and crying and hugging each other.

Just for one brief moment, Bunny and Claudine and I were one. For the last time.

'You're a funny sod, Ronnie,' gasped Bunny, weakly. 'Can't stand me one minute, save my life the next. I don't figure you at all.'

And then the ground crew came running.

They were married in the Roman Catholic church, that December. It was snowing. My father gave the bride away, and I was groomsman. Charlie Hill, who had bailed out, was best man. And Bunny limped up the aisle on a leg whose knee would never bend again. That was the reason he had not moved from his cockpit when the plane was burning; he couldn't move. He said it had hurt so much when I lifted him that he had nearly fainted. He said he would never be able to fly again.

So you might have thought they would have lived a peaceful married life. But I doubt it. We lost track of them, over the war years, as people did.

But when I was doing my basic training in the RAF in 1944, I saw a film of the recapture of Paris, by the armoured free French forces of

Général Lattre de Tassigny. And there, on the leading tank, amidst the snipers the Germans had left behind, sat a young woman in the black beret of the Resistance. I swear it was my Claudine. I mean, she was still wearing that ridiculous old sash, wasn't she?

Lulworth Cove

'Cool enough?' Martin's long-fingered hand fiddled again with the Merc's air-conditioning. The tiny zephyrs of coolness that played round Janice's face altered subtly.

'Lovely, thanks.' Again, she scuffed her feet luxuriously on the deep pile of the carpet, and settled her bottom into the broad seat. It was a lovely car. So why did she find the smell of leather so over-powering? Why did the view through the windscreen, with its single huge wiper, seem no more real than something on the telly? Why did she keep remembering with longing last summer in Dad's old Cortina, with all the windows down, and a gale blowing through the car, and the kids flying streamers with outstretched arms?

Martin was a super driver; she felt ever so safe with him. He hardly seemed to touch the controls; except the buttons that altered the wing mirrors. Martin was Junior Partner. Loaded. Knew how to show a girl a good time. Weekends in Paris, weeks in the Bahamas. Or so the girls round the office said. Charming. As long as he got his own way.

'I think we'll miss out Lulworth,' said Martin. 'You don't mind, do you? Tourist-trap. Jeff Edwards went there with his in-laws last summer. Said it was awful.'

'It *is* part of Hardy's Wessex,' said Janice, daring her first defiance. 'Only Hardy called it "Lulwind", not "Lulworth". It's where Sergeant Troy had his last swim in *Far From the Madding Crowd*.'

'Really?' said Martin, coldly, turning the Merc left at the next signpost for Lulworth. She had put him in a mood now. But a girl had to start as she meant to go on. And she knew plenty of ways of getting him out of it. It would be a shame to spoil their first weekend on the first day.

She glanced to the right as they ran down the narrow, green valley. A hump of cliff, unbelievably steep, like a roof, shot up into the sky, with tiny groups of people straggling up it, helping each other, like something out of *Pilgrim's Progress*. A signpost with crooked lettering and a pointing finger said 'To Durdle Door'. You just couldn't get a name more Thomas Hardy than Durdle Door. The cliff and its name sent little shivers of excitement up her spine.

But even she had to admit the car park was truly awful; a dreadful square hacked from the body of the little green valley. A huge area of cracked earth, dried-out runnels and blowing dust, which must once have been several pretty little fields. Rank upon rank upon rank of dusty cars and campers, like the parked panzers of an invading army.

The enormous notices that lined it were awful too.

HOT MEALS AT THE COVE RESTAURANT ALL THE TIME.

She had a vision of an endless expanse of fast food, as wide and arid as the car park, that seemed a desecration of time itself. No matter what the hour, brisk breakfast or leisurely lunch, stately tea or romantic dinner, the Cove Restaurant would just go on pouring out calories. Even in the middle of the night?

The second notice was four times the size, and even worse.

CLIFF CLIMBING IS DANGEROUS.
IT CAUSES DEATH EVERY YEAR.

It seemed to Janice not a caring notice, but an angry one. As if the cliff-climbing deaths were not a tragedy but merely a nuisance, a wretched loss of tourist revenue, an impediment to the serving of meals at the Cove Restaurant. She almost said to Martin, 'OK, you're right, let's go.'

But by that time he'd bought a car park ticket. He said crossly, 'It's a rip-off. One pound twenty, no matter how short your stay. But they've got us by the short and curlies. There's nowhere else to park. Even the double yellow lines have double yellow lines.'

Now they would have to stay, whether she liked it or not. Martin would insist on getting his money's worth, even if he hated everything.

'Can we look at the antique shop?' she asked, a little timidly. 'I love antiques.'

Inside the shop, Martin moved swiftly from object to object; picked up a brass door-stop and turned it over. His lip curled, when he saw it had a shiny back.

'Repro.'

He peered at Chinese paintings of cranes and goldfish.

'Best Taiwan, circa 1990.'

All round the crowded shop he went, uttering louder and louder grunts of disgust, till people began to turn and stare. 'All repro. Rubbish. Laid out to catch the mugs.' The shopkeeper began throwing him dirty looks, but Martin didn't even notice.

It was at this point that she saw the piggie teapot. A teapot in the form of a pig standing upright, dressed in a Victorian cook's uniform, even down to the little cap perched on her head. All in bright pink.

She remembered it was Vicky's birthday soon. Vicky adored pigs; Vicky collected novelty teapots. She would be delighted with it. Janice reached for her purse and caught the shopkeeper's eye.

'You're not buying *that* thing?' asked Martin, appearing at her elbow. 'Ten quid, and not even an antique?'

There seemed to be three people watching Janice now. Martin, outraged, imperious. The shopkeeper with a look of weary patience on his face. And, in Janice's mind, Vicky looking alternately hopeful and delighted. They were like a jury, coming to judgement.

'Ooooo-oh,' said Janice finally. 'I don't think I'll bother after all, thank you. I'd have to send it by post, and it would probably get broken.'

The shopkeeper turned away, tight-lipped. Vicky looked terribly sad and betrayed. Martin had already wandered off to sneer at something else.

But Janice found it hard to be angry for long in this tiny valley. It was so ingenious, the way the narrow road and the little clear-running stream twisted round each other, by means of little bridges, in the confined space. There were real weather-beaten fishing-boats parked upside down in the long grass of front gardens; beside tall piles of bleached lobster-pots with poles sticking out of the top on which flags of black plastic fluttered bravely in the breeze.

And the very old cat sitting on the low stone garden wall of the hotel. As Janice bent to stroke it, she noticed it was quite blind, from the thick blue film over its eyes. As it rose up to her stroking hand, she felt how frighteningly thin it was, under its fur; and how very stiff from arthritis. But Janice thought it was wonderful, the way it still found its way to its spot on the wall, to bask in the warmth of the sun and the love of the visitors, nearly all of whom stopped to stroke it. It was wonderful to Janice, almost holy, the way it trusted people in its last extremity and was not let down. Tears clouded her own eyes. Then she sensed Martin darken the sun behind her.

'Disgusting,' said Martin. 'A misery to itself and everybody else. Should have been put down months ago.'

'Wait till you're old and blind . . .'

Her sudden flare of anger took Martin by surprise. He gaped at her, and then said pompously, 'I don't intend to live that long. Want a drink? This hotel looks bearable.'

'No, thanks,' said Janice, even though she felt quite thirsty. She stalked off on stiff, indignant legs.

Across the road there was a pond with ducks; and little islands for them to nest on, made of rusting old lobster-pots and coils of bleached rope. Janice loved the sleek jolliness of ducks. Ducks were never sad and disillusioned; always seemed to enjoy life, with their little, twitching, curly tails . . .

'Mallards,' said Martin in disgust. 'Mallards are ten a penny. Why don't they get some real ornamental ducks? I can show you a place where they've got Mandarins and Muscovies, widgeon, goldeneye, scaup . . .'

'I *like* mallards,' gritted Janice. 'I like the way their tails twitch.' Which was pretty moderate of her, considering she really felt like telling him where he could *stuff* his Mandarins and Muscovies. She might still have done so, if there hadn't been a shout from behind them.

'Mind your backs!'

Four bronzed, near-naked, young men, running down to the beach carrying a huge black inflatable boat. From their short, bristly haircuts, strokeable as a mole's back, and their gloriously tattooed and bulging muscles, Janice was proud to deduce they must be soldiers in spite of their nudity. Soldiers laughing and whooping like Greek gods from the beginning of the world. Running to the sea like children on the first day of their holiday.

'Yobs,' remarked Martin loudly. But by then they were too far off to hear.

They carried on towards the sea. Now there was a big frail hut on the right, labelled powerfully but crudely.

THE STORY OF LULWORTH.

She cocked one eyebrow mockingly and indicated it with a sweeping gesture.

'Why not?' said Martin bitterly, and followed her inside.

She was entranced by the displays. A hundred million years of Lulworth. Eocene, Oligocene, Pleistocene, icthyosaurs and brontosaurs, ammonites and belemnites. She had always been an eager but erratic scholar. How strange time was! Dinosaurs had roamed where ice-cream carts now trundled in this same narrow valley. Ammonites had flourished where children now sucked in huge mouthfuls of candy floss.

'Have you seen *this*?' came Martin's outraged voice. 'And *this*?' He was pointing a trembling finger at Garfield the cartoon cat confronting several brontosaurs. And then at a fish-tank full of richly waving sea-anenomes that had as an underwater centrepiece a sunken model treasure-galleon in blue plastic, spilling forth its broken glinting treasure-chests.

'It's for the children,' she snapped. 'Weren't you ever a child?'

'This is supposed to be a serious exhibition!'

'Why does it have to be *serious*?'

People were starting to look at them. She turned her back on him and swept out. She felt like running away, but instead she walked very fast towards the shore. Why did he have to spoil *everything*?

She didn't stop, as she would have liked to have done, to speak to the laughing teenage girl cradling a tiny kitten in her arms. Or the gypsy-looking woman buying cakes for her clipped pug dog at a kiosk, and saying loudly, 'They must be macaroons! He won't eat anything but macaroons!'

They were all part of that glorious muddle called life; but Martin's non-stop vituperative tongue would kill them dead.

And so she came to the shore of the cove at last, and stood spellbound. At the raw-red strata of the rocks that heaved out of the sea in a giant loop; and another, and another. It was as if some giant child-god, a million years ago, had been rumpling an enormous piece of carpet and suddenly been called home to tea by his mother, and never returned. Nothing of note had happened since; the sticks and stones of man were no more than dust motes on that ancient rumpled carpet. Everything was *reduced*; even the waters of the cove, to a pellucid oyster-shell of pale blue light, on which a red-sailed yacht tacked backwards and forwards like a modern child's toy.

The modern works of man looked old and dusty and faded; the ancient power of the heaving rock was as new and raw as if it had happened yesterday.

Time, time, time, she thought. What was time, that leaned on your senses like some giant bully's hand? What are *we*? No more than this year's grass, already fading on the foreshore . . .

'Sordid, isn't it?' Martin had caught up with her again.

'*What*?' She nearly yelled at him, in her rage.

'All these bloody people . . . do they call this *enjoyment*?'

She looked at the people, and then she laughed. For every inch of the foreshore beach, concrete steps, upturned boats, launching-ramps, drying nets, was covered with close-packed bodies engaged in all manner of occupations. Young girls in bikinis sunbathed, while stout fathers bearing trays of tea from the kiosks stepped gingerly within inches of their heads. Children played with spinning tops and model yachts between the outstretched legs of kissing lovers. Men read newspapers while their sons leaned against their shoulders and attempted to fly kites. Two plump housewives in sunglasses shared the gunwhale of a fishing-boat with an old fisherman who was mending his nets as if they weren't there, but who, from the smile on his face, was enjoying their gossip.

All dwelling in their private worlds so politely, a matter of milli-metres apart. In its way, it was as big a miracle as the giant loops of rock; a very English miracle. The French would have been boasting to each other; the Italians might have squabbled; the Germans made a play for more *lebensraum*. But the English lived and let live, in most cosy privacy.

'God, what a *dump*!' said Martin. 'Let's go!'

She was far ahead of him, striding back up the little road, when she saw the little ramshackle hut marked 'Fortune-Teller' in garish and straggly lettering.

She could never, afterwards, quite work out why she went in. Was it just to *show* him, proclaim her independence? Or did she need to find some mystery in Lulworth, that he kept cutting her off from?

The moment she stepped through the door, she wished she hadn't. But she wasn't going to back down now, not with him hurrying up behind and watching her. She sat down opposite the woman, on a rickety chair in front of a rickety bamboo table.

It was unbelievable. The woman actually said, 'Cross my palm with silver,' though she immediately added something about, 'Five pounds,' after it.

Janice fumbled in her bag for the five-pound note, bitterly regretting her own stupidity. It wasn't just the five pounds wasted. It wasn't just that Martin had come up and was glaring at her through the window. It was that, to escape being in the power of a man, she had put herself in the power of a woman.

Not a very nice-looking woman either. Her eyes were bright and intelligent, but also small and mean. And her white hair, held back with a lot of half-lodged hairpins, needed washing. In fact, in that hot little cabin of thin wood, she positively *smelled*.

The woman took her hand, palm upwards and scrutinised it with her head on one side, as a lawyer might scrutinise a will, or a doctor an X-ray. God, they were all the same these people, Janice thought with disgust. They love their little bit of power, of drama. Then the woman said, 'You're going to marry a farmer, and have three children.'

It was all so *ridiculous*. Janice said, quite rudely for her, 'I don't *know* any farmers. How could I meet any farmers? I work in the City and I live in a flat in Docklands. My parents live in West Ham . . . I've never met a farmer in my life.' She glanced out of the window, at Martin, as if seeking for reassurance of how ridiculous this woman was being.

The woman followed her eyes, and saw Martin.

'You won't marry *him*,' she said spitefully.

'How can you possibly know that?' asked Janice. Starting to mock her, now.

The woman's eyes looked at her, very sharp. 'Because he don't listen to a thing you say. Because you see things, and he don't. And you try an' show him, an' he won't even try to see them.'

That shook Janice. It was like a spear going home into her heart, it was so true. But then she got a grip on herself, and told herself that the woman must have watched them go past before, quarrelling. That was all it was. The woman was sharp, she watched people, made deductions like a smart detective, and then pretended it was magic.

The woman said, 'I'll tell 'ee more. 'Ee was goin' into Devon wi' that feller, for the weekend. Well 'ee'll never get to Devon. Ee'll be home in London by tonight, and ee'll never see that feller again, after that.'

'What utter rubbish.' Janice got up, preparing to go.

But the old woman reached over and grabbed her wrist; her grip was cold and thin, like the claw of a bird that perches on your hand; but surprisingly powerful.

'Let go of me!' shouted Janice, starting to struggle. But somehow she couldn't shake off the hand; not without it getting undignified, or risking hurting the old woman.

'You think I'm an old fool, don't you? An old fool that knows nothing? I'll show you. My name's Emily Routledge and it's known round these parts; I'll show you that Emily Routledge knows more than you think. See this?'

With her other hand she held up something small and round and gold that winked in one of the few beams of sunlight that filtered into the cabin. 'That's a sovereign, a real gold sovereign – Queen Victoria's head on it and not a bite mark in it. Mint-perfect. I took that into a jeweller's in Weymouth an' he told me it was worth two hunnerd pound. It was my granny's, she left it me, but I'll give it to you on one condition . . .'

She twisted it this way and that, in a way that almost hypnotised Janice.

'Ee likes gold, don't 'ee?' asked the old woman slyly. Which gave Janice another start, for she did. Until she remembered that at that very moment she was wearing a gold chain that Martin had just given her, and three gold bracelets from her last boyfriend.

'Why will you give it to me?' she asked the woman.

'To prove I'm right. I'll give it to 'ee if you can get that feller out there to come in here and see me and collect it for you. That's my only condition. He's got to come in here and see me by himself, and I'll give it him for you.'

'And what do *you* get out of it?'

'Proof that I'm right, when he won't come. When you've coaxed him and pleaded till you're blue in the face, and he still won't come to please you, then you come back and tell old Emily that she was right an' you was wrong . . .'

'Done,' said Janice. Sure of her power over men. I'll show you, you old fool.

They glared at each other for a moment. Janice could almost feel pity for the old woman, with her wrinkled eyes, and the little straggle of grey hairs under her chin. It must be sad to be so old and ugly and unwanted. She felt sorry for her, till she looked her in the eyes. Eyes bright and alert and knowing, without emotions, like the eyes of a lizard.

Then the woman let go her hand, and she blundered out.

'What on earth were you . . .?' Martin was very, very angry. It narrowed his mouth, and his eyes, and made him look mean. Which was the last thing he was really, as all the girls said.

But Janice just smiled at him, her slowest, warmest, laziest smile, her own eyes half-closed, and put her finger across his lips.

'C'mon. I'll let you buy me that drink now. I've got an interesting story for you . . .'

And after a long pause he gave up his right to be angry, though he said, 'You women are the scattiest, most feather-brained things . . .' He went on lecturing her all the way to the hotel; but she kept on squeezing his hand, in that special way, and all the heat went out of his lecturing, till he finally said, 'You are a sexy old thing.'

She let him put his arm round her, to guide her into the hotel. Let him choose where they would sit, let him boss the waiter about. She knew all these things helped to soothe him down. She was good with men. She played footsie-footsie with him under the table, while they waited for the drinks to come. Didn't say a thing until, restored, he said indulgently, 'What's this interesting story you've got for me?'

He treasured her interesting stories, her carefully chosen supply of office gossip. She knew he told the stories as his own, at board meetings, that he used the gossip to give his fellow directors the impression he had his ear to the ground, when really he was so full of himself and his own ideas he was almost blind to the people who worked around him.

She paused, till she had his full attention, till the drinks had come, and he had tried his own and pronounced it OK, then she said, 'That strange old woman offered me a mint Queen Victoria sovereign.'

'How much?' How quickly his face changed, how his eyes narrowed! And she suddenly realised how often, in conversation, his question was 'how much?'.

'Nothing,' she said, and giggled.

'*Nothing*!' Then a slight look of anxiety crossed his face. 'You're having me on.' How terrified he was of looking a fool! What a need he had to be the knowing, worldly-wise man. The man who might buy a new Merc without blinking, but only after he'd searched the whole city to find the firm who gave the biggest discount for cash.

'No, honest, she offered me this sovereign for nothing. She showed it to me. It was perfect. It had been her granny's.'

'What's the catch?' How often was that his question? What's the catch? He saw life as a minefield.

'The only catch is that somebody else has got to go and fetch it for me. Isn't that a *scream*? I've got to find somebody else who likes me enough to fetch it for me.'

'But . . . they wouldn't have to *like* you. You could pay them to do it. I'll tip this waiter . . . it won't take him a minute.'

He turned in his armchair, to summon the waiter, a five-pound note magically already in his hand.

'No,' she said, taking a deep breath. 'It has to be you. She said it had to be my feller waiting outside. *You* have to go in and fetch it for me.'

'Me? You must be joking!' But he knew she wasn't joking. Distaste wrinkled his nose, revulsion even. But in his eyes there was a little spark of fear.

'Go on,' she said. 'It won't take a minute. You just said so. You could be back with it, before I'd had two sips of my drink.'

'You . . . really . . . expect *me* to go over there? To go into that smelly hutch, with that smelly old hag?' He said it with such hate. Janice wondered with a shiver whether she would ever become a smelly old hag? Whether he would ever say it about *her*?

'Maybe I'll be a smelly old hag myself, one of these days.'

She enjoyed his little flinch.

'You couldn't ever get like that!' he said, after a moment.

'Thank you for that belated vote of confidence.' Her tongue was getting sharper than she meant. Then she launched into her first lie.

'She said if you loved me enough, you'd fetch it for me.' He was silent, playing with his glass, rolling the base of it round and round on the table. After a while she added, with half-suppressed rage, 'You mean you *don't* love me enough?'

'I don't believe she would give it to me, even if I went.'

'You mean you don't believe a thing I tell you?'

'Oh, come off it, Janice. I believe everything you tell me. Except this. This is *ridiculous*.'

'You mean *I'm* being ridiculous.'

'Yes, if you like. I mean, if you want a damned sovereign so much, we can call in at some jeweller's in Weymouth and I'll *buy* you one. You can't say I'm mean . . .' His eyes drifted, a little smugly, she thought, to the chain round her neck. As if he not only owned it, but her.

'*Hers* has got Queen Victoria on it.'

'For Christ's sake! OK. When we get back, Monday morning, I'll ring somebody in Hatton Garden. We'll *get* you a Queen Victoria.'

'Anything that money can buy, in fact!'

'All right. Anything that money can buy.' Then he added, 'Within reason.' Which made her give a little bitter smile, which hurt her even more than it hurt him.

'But you won't go into a smelly hutch for me? For two minutes? It isn't even a matter of getting your hands dirty.'

'What's so important about my getting my hands dirty? I got them dirty enough on that management survival course on the Isle of Skye.'

'But that was approved dirt – dirt the firm had paid for.'

'What the hell are we arguing about dirt for?'

'We are not arguing about dirt. We are arguing about that old hag sitting over there, loving it, loving knowing that she was right about you and I was wrong.' Janice was close to tears now.

'What the hell are you crying for? Are you mad or something?'

She picked up her handbag and walked out. Before anybody else noticed her crying. Crying not with sadness, but with pain, rage . . .

He ran after her. He did not give up that easily, for she was very beautiful and he wanted her very much. They walked, walked the cliff paths, tearing each other to ribbons, while the Merc waited in the carpark, and the five-star hotel in Torbay waited in vain for their coming.

This is so *stupid*, she thought, every time they passed the carpark. We could be away and laughing.

But the grim old woman and the sovereign held her like a hook in a fish's mouth. The grim old woman who looked up and smiled every time they passed.

And then came the time, towards dusk, when she looked through the window of the cabin, and saw the old woman was no longer there, and it all no longer mattered.

'Take me home,' she said abruptly. 'To London.'

And so the first of the old woman's forecasts came true.

After that, it became uncanny. She couldn't possibly stay with the firm, where she might see him every day. And she knew her career prospects there were in ruins. Worse, she somehow dare not ask the firm for a reference.

She went temping. And, in the fullness of time, for her seventh or her seventeenth temping job, she found herself by chance working at the Agricultural Institute, attached to the University of London. And they offered her a full-time job (as all the others had, because she was good). But becoming desperate at her rootlessness, and remembering

Lulworth, she took this one. Why not? Nothing would happen, of course . . .

Robin Moresby came to the Institute, to give a lecture on his new lamb-rearing methods. He saw her, and like so many young men before him, he asked her for a date.

And again, she said why not? What had she got to lose?

He was harmless. And amusing. And respectful. Not a pusher. When he asked her down for a weekend at his parents' house, she accepted quite gaily. A lovely old half-timbered farmhouse, a big farm. Robin ran a slightly smaller one, next door. It was all gentle, restful, comfortable.

When he finally asked her to marry him, she said, why not?

Robin, snub-nosed, red-haired Robin, never quite got over his luck at acquiring a lovely girl like that. He spoilt her rotten, bought her red roses when their first child was born.

And the second. And the third! It all seemed to pass in a dream, a happy dream . . .

It took the phone call from Martin to move her. He rang up late one night. Told her what trouble he'd gone to, to trace her. He talked interminably. He was still unmarried. And very, very drunk. She was thirty by that time. He was over forty, and kept on weeping about it. He had never forgotten her; he had decided she was the only one for him.

She told him to get lost and hung up, shaking from head to foot.

That was the night she decided to go back to Lulworth Cove. To tell the fortune-teller she was right.

She had to wait till the lambing season was over. Then they all packed into the Volvo, with Stephen, aged six, young Robin, aged four and Vivian, aged three, in the back.

Only on the way there did she tell Robin about the fortune-teller. In his steady, amused way, he was impressed.

'Bit of luck for me, old thing. I can see it all now. Did wonder at the time what a lovely girl like you saw in a country bumpkin like me. Bit of a pushover, you were. I couldn't believe my luck. Didn't get a wink of sleep till I got you to the altar . . .' He gave her an affectionate squeeze. Which she liked.

The fortune-teller wasn't there. Even the hut where she'd sat was gone. Janice felt a terrible emptiness which she could never have believed possible, married to Robin.

And Robin felt what she was feeling. Took her back to the carpark, saw her comfortable with a cup of tea from a flask, and took the kids off for a walk round the village, young Vivian riding gaily on his shoulders.

She wondered about the passing of time, and her life, and dozed and dreamed of dinosaurs.

He seemed to be back in no time, though she looked at her watch as she heard their voices approaching, and saw that two hours had passed.

Robin opened the door and gave her a disarming shrug. 'Made a few inquiries round the village. No luck, I'm afraid.'

But he'd reckoned without the thirst for truth of his eldest son.

'Dadd-ee, stop telling whoppers! They said that fortune-teller was a dreadful old nuisance and they chucked her out of the village after a week, 'cos she kept making people fed up with her rotten old gold.'

'Out of the mouths of babes and sucklings,' said Robin ruefully. 'I didn't know the little beggar had such sharp ears. Sorry, darling. Didn't want to upset you, but he's got the gist of it. She seems to have pulled that nasty sovereign trick on any number of people. Old charlatan!'

Janice thought of what might have been, and what was. Robin was just as real as the folding of the rocks and the dinosaurs, as the ice-cream carts and the candy floss.

She had her personal share of time and reality; and was content.

'Let's go home,' she said, and squeezed his brawny, hairy, lovely arm.

Fatty
France

Teachers were pretty neurotic about sex in the last war. We were supposed to be a mixed grammar school; but boys and girls were kept separate for the first three years.

Not that this worried us lads. In the corridors, every break and lunch-time, we elbowed our way past the cowering, cringing classes of girls. We thought nothing of them. We thought them a whingeing, ankle-socked, knobbly-kneed, be-hair-clipped lot. Any charms they might have had were buried inside voluminous gym tunics that would have buried the charms of Mae West and Betty Grable, who had her legs insured for a million dollars.

But it was a lark to lunge extra-hard with your elbow, and get an agonised squeak out of one of the pillow-like gym-slips, and a chorus of shrill indignant recrimination from her friends.

If you caught a glimpse of some pale and lovely profile in the shadows, you gave it no more attention than if it was a wild flower. Life for us lads was push, smash and bash, and the devil take the hindmost in a world full of punches in the guts and noses streaming blood and snot in the toilets.

Only the girl prefects were worthy of our attention; glorious in their striped blazers and thrusting blouses that showed faint ghosts of white bras underneath. Girl prefects could punish us. Oh, the *glory* of being punished by your favourite; to have to cross into the girls' half of the school and knock on their prefect's room door, and ask for her by name, and smell the female smell of their tiny hen-coop of wooden partitions.

Then, in the fourth year, we were pushed in with the girls. But segregation died hard. You might as well have cut that classroom in half with a knife. Boys grabbed the best half, by the windows. The girls complained we always did, but we just jeered, 'Come and chuck us out, then!'

The frontier between us was marked by empty desks; or desks full of girls of evil repute, who, it was rumoured, let lads *do* things to them, after dark, in side-alleys on the way home. Or desks full of dirty-minded boys who we despised, and showed our contempt for, by not laughing at their scruffy jokes.

But there was communication of sorts. Surreptitiously passed notes. The girls wrote theirs on coloured, scented notepaper; we just ripped pages out of our rough notebooks. We learned many things. First, the secret of the indecent writing in the school music books, which were given out to us for singing lessons only, then taken in again by the elderly music master, to be given out to the girls in turn.

Music lessons, in our first three years, had been sometimes halted for half an hour, while the music master made us search these books for dirty alterations in pencil. These we had to rub out thoroughly, lest, as the music master so often said, our male filth should soil the flower of English womanhood.

Not, I might add, that these alterations seemed very dreadful or corrupting to me. The worst I ever found was that someone had altered the title 'Cherry Ripe' to 'Cherry Tripe'. I pointed this out to the music master, with a tiny grin, implying it was not very serious. That was a mistake. He held my neck in a vice-like grip, while I rubbed and rubbed with my tiny precious rubber, until it went clean through the paper. And all the while he told me how vile I was, not to have thought it vile. He even speculated that I might have written it myself.

How strange to feel human madness for the first time, through the clench of the hand of authority on your neck! Like when the woodwork master gripped you for mis-measuring, and ruining a piece of 'good wood' in wartime. 'GOOOOD WOOOOOD,' he would warble, beating you over the head with the ruined piece. This was his only sign of life. For the rest of the time he would sit in the corner, reading the *Daily Telegraph*, his thin blue pinstriped legs protruding below. Goody Woody Chatwin we called him, and hurtled around the playground at break howling 'GOOOOOOOOOOD WOOOOOOOD!', and sounding like diving German Stukas. We accepted then that all our teachers were old, or mad, or both.

But I digress. What we now learned from the girls was that it was *they* who had written the dirty words in the music books. The flower of English womanhood had defiled itself. Which explained why, though the Music master watched us lads like hawks, none of us had ever been caught writing the stuff.

We made the delightful and liberating discovery that girls had *much* dirtier minds than boys. The jokes they passed us, on their scented notepaper, were much better and scruffier than ours. We also discovered they knew all the dirty bits in the Bible, Deuteronomy and so forth.

This inspired me to my first literary masterpiece. A fantasy sex-life of the staff, couched in Biblical language. 'And lo, the headmaster lay with the deputy headmistress, and she conceived in her womb and brought forth a two-headed goat.'

The trouble was, it was too good. The boys, who were used to my stuff, managed to keep straight faces, but the first girl just exploded like a giggle-bomb.

The teacher pounced, read. It was a terrible moment. Inside this class, she would be able to identify even my *printing*. Expulsion loomed. After six of the best from the Head. Oh, my parents, my poor, trusting parents, sitting all peaceful at home . . .

Except the girl who was caught with it, Stella France, stoutly avowed, under great and prolonged pressure, that she had picked it up in the school yard at break.

Now Stella France was a swot, a favourite of the teachers, a head girl of the future. She now had to stand, white and trembling, while she was told in front of us all how she had besmirched her own pure womanhood, the honour of the school, the good name of her parents. How she was undermining the British Empire in its darkest hour.

Then she was led away and given three of the best by the deputy headmistress, a white-haired dragon of fearful aspect called Laetitia Middleton MA (Cantab). Only female teachers were allowed to cane girls; ours was a civilised society. They used a thinner cane than the men; the girls said it cut deeper.

So Stella France lost her good name with the staff. And yet failed to get a good name among the boys. For though some said she had been brave and a good sport, most held that she was a dangerous fool to let herself get caught in the first place.

I caught up with her, walking home to lunch.

'Thanks a lot,' I mumbled at her highly polished feet.

'Thanks for nothing,' she said, her voice tight with pain and rage. 'I thought you would own up and save me. Like a *gentleman*.'

'They'd have caned us both, then. And *expelled* me.'

'They'd have been *justified*.'

I looked at her. She was nursing her painful left hand squeezed tight inside her right. There were tears in her large grey eyes, just brimming at the lids. Her mouth was as tight as a rat-trap, to stop herself crying. It shook me from head to foot that she had been wounded for my transgressions. I felt a sexy wriggle in my gut. I think I half fell in love with her then.

But it wasn't her physical pain she was nearly crying about.

'Miss Middleton's going to write to my mother. My good name's gone for good. I'm ruined. They'll *never* make me a prefect now.'

Oh, such proud beauty in distress!

'Sorry,' I said. And for once I must have looked it.

'You look like a kicked puppy-dog,' she said. Then added, with an attempt at a grin, 'It was a very funny story. You shouldn't be let loose on your own!'

'I'm going to be a famous writer when I grow up,' I said. I thought she might be interested.

Maybe she was, though she didn't say so. Whether it was that, or the pain I'd caused her I don't know, but she responded by asking me to her next birthday party.

She was the only girl I knew who could afford to have a big birthday party in wartime. God knew where her mother got the salmon and ham sandwiches, the tarts and shop cakes, the sherry trifle, but they were good. The grub was the main reason why us lads went, in our hairy and uncomfortable one-and-only best suits; scrubbed to a pink shine by our mothers and with our hair smarmed down with tap-water because we couldn't afford Brylcreem.

She lived in the posh private semis off Lansdowne Terrace. Funny, nearly all the girls lived in private semis, whereas us lads mainly lived on council estates, or in the rented terraces down by the river. As I walked down to her house, half terrified, my main worry was that I would never dare ask her or her mother where the loo was, if I needed to go. I mean, you could try and just slip out of the room where the party was, and explore the house till you found it. But you might blunder into her parents' bedroom by mistake, or meet them on the stairs, and they might think you were trying to nick something.

I had gone to the loo at the last possible moment. And resolved not to drink a drop until I got home again. But I kept on thinking about it, and when you have thought about it long enough, it starts to tickle and you know you have to go, even if you don't really need to.

Her mother opened the door. I didn't dare look her in the face, but she was wearing a nice dress.

'Leave your coat in here,' she said. 'And if you'd like to wash your hands, the bathroom's upstairs and first on the right.'

Wash my hands *again*? I'd washed them three times before I set out, and they were still slightly damp and very white from the last time. This was slanderous, not to be borne. I held them up for her inspection, as if she was the school nurse or something: 'Quite clean, thank you!'

Only then, when I had made a total idiot of myself, did I realise that where the bathroom was, there would be the toilet also. The blood rushed up my face to the roots of my hair, and I dived blindly towards the sound of female party-giggles.

The girls were there, all seven of them. No boys yet. Oh, God, had I come to the wrong room? But the girls were advancing on me. Gone were the gym slips and grey ankle socks and knobbly white knees. Legs gleamed shapely in stockings above high-heeled shoes; party-dresses revealed curves unguessed-at. Lipstick, perfume. All the weapons of grown-up women, and armed with such weapons, they seemed filled with demonic self-confidence. Like our rugby-pack coming on to the field against Tynemouth School, who we always beat thirty-five-nil.

I had been expecting that we would play, at this party, the good old games we played at family Christmas parties. Waft the Kipper, Hunt the Thimble, Banging Balloons Against the Ceiling.

Somehow I realised it was not going to be that kind of party.

I was right. Instead of Musical Chairs, we had Musical Knees. Us lads sat, stolid and unmoving, trying to keep our dignity, while soft young bottoms thumped down on us, shapely young thighs wrapped themselves round ours, shapely young arms embraced us. The grumpier we looked, the funnier they thought it was. But Musical Knees wasn't the worst. That was called Winkie. The girls sat on a circle of chairs, facing inwards. The boys stood behind the chairs. One boy had an empty chair. He was supposed to wink secretly at one of the sitting girls. She was supposed to make a dive for his chair, evading the arms of the boy behind her, who tried to stop her escaping. If she made it, she kissed her new boy; if she didn't, she had to kiss her old boy, who had caught her in time. That was the way it should have worked, if the girls had played fair.

But they didn't. If you winked at them, and they didn't fancy you, they ignored your wink, making you feel about an inch high. Or else they'd try to escape so slowly that their old boy would catch them over and over, and they'd have an orgy of kissing, which made you feel like committing axe-murder.

It rapidly sorted out the desirable from the undesirable. A sort of sexual Olympic Games. Or a sexual Olympic blood-sport that could rip your ego down to the bare and bleeding bone.

Hopefully, I tried one wink at our Stella. She blatantly ignored me. She was after Ian Smith, the bitch. Making eyes at him, *inviting* him.

Right, here was me opting out! There were two girls who'd never had a wink at all. One was a quite good-looking girl called Jane, who had the unfortunate habit of scratching herself in embarrassing places without noticing what she was doing. Decent upright lads steered clear of that sort of thing. Including me; it could get you talked about for six months afterwards, if you went anywhere near her.

The other was a thin girl with a friendly horsey face, and the unfortunate name of Mollie Nattrass. All the boys called her Nattrass the Mattress, because nobody had the least desire to lie down on top of her.

I opted for Nattrass the Mattress. Like a darling, she came. I kissed her quite warmly out of sheer gratitude for filling my empty chair and my despairing heart. In return, she let me catch her when Spotty Hargreaves winked at her in turn. Oh, bliss, Nattrass the Mattress preferred me to Spotty Hargreaves! Down you go, Hargreaves, straight into the hell of the unloved and unwanted! I'm all right, Jack, I am in the dinghy!

Nattrass the Mattress and I saw each other safe through the final and most diabolical game, which rightly was called Murder. It was only really hide and seek played in pairs, one boy, one girl. What the other couples got up to in the kitchen broom cupboard, and Stella's mother's wardrobe, I never found out, let alone what Spotty Hargreaves and the Unfortunate Scratcher got up to in the hall chest. But in the linen cupboard upstairs, Nattrass the Mattress and I conversed about films we'd seen, in discreet whispers. I told her my favourite film star was Ingrid Bergman, and she told me hers was Gary Cooper. We were so discreet we actually won the game and got a prize each. Bars of chocolate, too, when it was on ration; great big bars! Mutual friendship blossomed under such prosperity. We always smiled at each other after that, whenever we met in the school corridor. But I never took her out, even when later she got much curvier and better-looking. You *couldn't* take out somebody called Nattrass the Mattress. Life would not have been worthwhile, once back among the lads. You'd have had to hit too many people, for asking too many leading questions.

Meanwhile, I settled down to making Stella France pay the price for humiliating me at Winkie. There was only one way to do it. Schoolwork. She was top of the class that term, and I was only fifth, because I was lazy and only did well at subjects I liked. But it was fairly easy to beat her the following term, because she was already an out-and-out swot, and I was an undiscovered genius. She would always be best at French and Latin, but I could write good essays, none better. So all I had to do was start caring about crummy things like music and RE. My trump-card was art. She was hopeless at art and there, too, my genius showed. She said that art shouldn't be counted as an exam subject, because it was a God-given gift. I told her to God-given Get Lost. When, at the end of that term, they announced I was top, and she was only second, I think I caught a satisfying glint of tears in her eyes, a tightness of the mouth. What I didn't reckon with was the queer effect that humiliation can have on a female. I think she must have fallen in love with me then. She took to giving me long soulful looks across the classroom, but as I was not co-operating (having not forgotten the party) there wasn't a lot else she could do about it.

Except one thing. Under her sufferings, she seemed to blossom. Her legs had become worth watching some time before. Now she blossomed up-top too. It was a pity that, although she played tennis for the school, and won, she was a bit too thick about the waist. It was about then, at the time of her blossoming, that the lads in our class began to call her Fatty. It was very unfair, really. But I enjoyed the unfairness. That would teach her to act stuck-up! That would teach her to give me long lingering looks across the classroom!

And then she pulled the fast one. Maybe she'd been talking about me to Nattrass the Mattress; maybe Nattrass the Mattress had told her how gone I was on Ingrid Bergman the film star. That was at the time when Ingrid Bergman appeared in the film of *For Whom the Bell Tolls* with her hair cut very short and boyish.

Fatty France had her hair cut the same way. And it bloody worked. She did look just like Ingrid Bergman, same up-tilted nose, same lovely cheekbones and big grey eyes. Same soft bloom on her cheeks. It was agonising.

But it still didn't do her any good. For one excellent reason. Until then, I'd been called Fatty Donaldson. I'd been fat lower down the school, but recently it had all turned to muscle. Honest, I was six feet high, and only weighed twelve stone and was in the running for the school rugby team as wing forward. But the name stuck. Like the jokes would stick, if Fatty Donaldson went out with Fatty France. Questions about how the act of love might be achieved.

There matters stuck, while we walked into the execution block of the School Certificate exams.

That September she walked into the sixth with seven As and a B. I walked in with eight As and a failure. Latin. I think it must have driven her mad with passion.

But it was a passion that might well have gone unrequited, except that at that time, my father joined the Freemasons, which wasn't important, and my mother was thus entitled to join the Order of the Eastern Star, which was.

Because Mrs France was already a member of the Eastern Star. And, as we said in those days, she made herself known to my mother, in the most pleasant way, by asking if my mother was the mother of a genius named Donaldson in the sixth form at the high school, of whom her daughter was always talking . . .

I was not exactly displeased at this. I was going on like a genius in English lessons, because now we were not just having facts stuffed down us, we were being asked our opinions too. I was long and strong on opinions; whereas most of the class, even Stella, were still sitting like stuffed ducks but taking lots of notes about what the teacher and I said.

I was enjoying the sixth form a lot; except the Latin, which I had to have, if I was going to read English at university. I mean, the Latin set books were really horrible. I didn't mind Caesar and his neat little ablative absolute (I even took to using the ablative absolute in English, much to the teacher's rage). I didn't even mind good old Virgil, with his *Sic fatur lacrimans*. But Livy, with those incredible long sentences, where you had to search for the main verb in the middle of the next page . . .

It was then that the cunning Fatty France made her most deadly move. My mother came home from a meeting of the Eastern Star one night, and she was no longer wearing the satisfied smirk of the mother of a genius. She had a face as dark as thunder.

Mrs France had told her that Stella was deeply worried about my progress in Latin. I was getting terrible marks, and if I didn't improve, I would ruin my whole career . . .

An atmosphere descended that made the Nuremberg Trials sound like a teddy-bear's picnic. I squawked and wailed and protested louder than Herman Goering. But it was no use. Mrs France was not only in the Eastern Star, she was the deputy madam chairwoman of the Eastern Star. She lived in a private semi. Her husband was an officer, still in the RAF in Germany. She was rather more important than King George the Sixth; one down from God. If she said I was going to fail, I was going to fail.

I spent a long time promising amendment of life, as the Bible puts it, and cursing the sneaky ways of Fatty France. What a small-minded, petty, *pointless* revenge! Even though I was full of rage, I also felt a pitying contempt at the *feebleness* of it, the self-destructiveness of it. It was worthy of Bill Berry, the sixth form Total Bastard, who spent his spare time pulling wings off flies. Was she trying to *scare* me into falling in love with her?

I spent the next fortnight ignoring Fatty as if she was gone from the face of the earth. Though I went out of my way to be totally charming to every other girl in the set. But she didn't seem unduly worried by this. It was as if she was waiting for something, brooding over some future triumph.

It was not long in coming. My mother returned from the next meeting of the Eastern Star beaming all over her face. Disaster was averted; Stella France had offered to coach me in Latin at home, over the Easter holidays, she was so worried for me.

I did my roaring Herman Goering act all over again, but it was quite useless. The kindness, thoughtfulness and general divinity of the France family was extolled; my sheer ingratitude held up before me as the blackest of crimes. I was not only ungrateful, I was unnatural. And if I didn't go down to the France house pronto as soon as the Easter weekend was over, they would take me away from school when I failed my Latin exam that summer, and I'd be forced into a wretched clerk's job at Smith's Dock . . .

I went with hate in my heart. She opened the front door wearing high heels and nylons, lipstick and powder, looking more like Ingrid Bergman than ever.

The Latin books were ready on the table, open. She took me through three pages of Livy in three hours, and at the end I hated Livy even more. Not that she didn't know her stuff. But we had to work close; fingers touched, I smelled the smell of her hair, of her perfume.

She crossed her legs and I watched her knees . . . who could concentrate on Livy? I dreamed of doing totally vile things to her, which I had only thought of before in connection with the unfortunate girls who were rumoured to let you do things to them on the playing-field after dark. But I played the perfect gentleman; only, the perfect gentleman who was so stupid at Latin, he'd even forgotten the meaning of *Ego sum*.

At four o'clock, her mother bustled in with a nice little tray of tea, with bought cakes again. I ate three cakes out of the four, after she had coyly refused her second, saying she had to watch her figure . . . I made a non-stop speech, full of cake crumbs, about the pointlessness of Latin in the modern world, and my new-found desire to take up art as a career, because art was the one course you could do at university that didn't need Latin.

She let me finish, then said with a steely glance, 'Same time tomorrow?'

Tomorrow turned out to be much the same. Both my Latin and my fantasies grew worse. We had more of the same cakes. They were getting a bit stale, but I still munched my way through three. I might as well get something out of it.

Halfway through my repeat speech on the pointlessness of Latin, her mother came back for the tray and sensed the atmosphere, and said, with a falsely bright smile, 'All work and no play makes Jack a dull boy. Why don't the pair of you go out tomorrow, if it's fine? On your bikes?'

What could I say, but yes?

We went to Holywell Dene some five miles away. A deep green gorge full of huge green trees just coming out into leaf. I don't know why I took her to Holywell Dene, except that I always went there when I went for a bike-ride. It was the place I'd had most fun as a kid. Camping, fires, blackened roast spuds in the embers . . .

I heaved our bikes over the fence, and hid them in the bramble-bushes at the top of the bank, to stop them being stolen by thieving kids, like we always did. Then I turned to her and said, 'Come on! I'll show you the stream that runs along the bottom; it's black with coal-dust from the colliery at Barsdon. It's really funny, all the place is so green and lovely, and yet the stream runs black.' I mean, I felt I had to show her something; it was what you showed people when you first took them to Holywell Dene.

She hesitated in the sunlight, at the edge of the tree-shadow. She was wearing a snazzy pair of shorts, which showed off her legs a treat. Her blue aertex shirt, with little dark patches of sweat under her armpits, didn't do her any harm either. Her hair was freshly cut and washed, and she looked more like Ingrid Bergman than ever. So what was she hesitating like that for? As if she was afraid of the place.

'Nowt to worry about,' I said. 'Only a few rabbits, and you see fox-cubs sometimes. No lions or tigers!'

She gave me a wide-eyed look of near terror. What the hell was she scared of?

And then it hit me like a thunderbolt.

She was scared of *me*. Her mother must have told her all about the wicked ways of lads, when they got girls in lonely, quiet places. She thought *I* was the tiger; that I was going to leap on her and rape her, as soon as we got past the first set of screening bushes.

The shock of it nearly knocked me senseless. I had never leaped on anybody like a tiger in my life. Except Bill Berry on the rugby field, after he and his mates had been particularly unpleasant about me living on a council estate. And what happened to Bill Berry was not what she had in mind.

It irritated me, to think that she thought I was that kind of guy. I would show her how very far I was from being that kind of guy. Except in my fantasies, and that was different. Fantasies never hurt anybody . . .

'C'mon,' I said brutally. 'We haven't got all day.'

And that was the amazing thing. She thought she was going to be leaped on and raped, and she still came. Slowly, wide-eyed, but she came. We walked between the silent coolness of the trees, and I pointed and said things like, 'That's the tree we used to swing on. We brought a rope and an old tyre from home, and played at Tarzan.'

'This is the campsite we usually use. Look, you can see the burnt patch still, in the turf.'

'Look, here's the river. Isn't it black? The sides are pure coal-dust.'

Each time she nodded, mutely. Like a Christian martyr awaiting the lions.

It was funny. Normally I found Holywell Dene fascinating, but it seemed quite boring that morning. There wasn't really anything of interest to show anybody.

Finally I said, in mild disgust, 'That's all there is, really. Just kid's stuff, really.' And led her back to the bikes.

I thought she would cheer up, then. Back to safety, unravished and all that. But she just seemed depressed. We didn't say much all the way home. I rode in front and she rode behind, and there were some steep hills that made us puff, and talking difficult.

We parted at the end of her street with a perfunctory wave. I rode home having the wildest fantasies about what I *might* have done to her. Anyway, I'd be seeing her again tomorrow. And after all my fantasies, I was quite looking forward, not to Livy, but to smelling the smell of her hair, and touching fingers.

Some hopes. When I got there the next day, her mother opened the door. She was sorry, but Stella was starting a cold. She didn't want to give it to me. Perhaps next week.

But I knew it was the brush-off. I would never be helped with my Livy again. I was back in some outer darkness. I had failed some test. She must have wanted to be leaped on.

That was the first time I realised I didn't really understand women.

Still, I did a lot of fantasising that holiday. Sometimes I was the villain, and sometimes the hero. In my fantasy, she seemed to like the villain much better.

The next meeting of the Eastern Star, Mrs France told my mother I was much improved in Latin, and could now safely manage on my own.

If only that had been true, how different my story might have been.

One of the insufferable things about Bill Berry was the way he had improved in Latin. He had failed it at O level, like me. But in the sixth form, he suddenly seemed to have got a lot better. We had things called 'unseens' where you had to translate a bit of Latin into English, for homework. And whereas I was getting about eighteen per cent for my unseens, and the girls like Stella France were getting about eighty, Berry was steadily getting seventy.

I was puzzled for a bit, and then by chance I found out how he was doing it. We didn't pass in the homework in class, you see. We left it on the Latin teacher's shelf outside the staff room. And I was just watching Berry leaving his on the shelf one day, with hate in my heart, when I saw that he went to the shelf with one exercise book, his own . . . and came away with two. He was nicking one of the books already passed in; one of the girls' books, no doubt. They always handed in their homework early . . . I watched him sneak off to an empty classroom and copy out the work quickly. Then he went and put both books back on the shelf. He was very clever at it; he just looked, both times, as if he was dithering, wool-gathering. No teacher would ever have suspected. He held the other book tightly under his own. If he'd been caught, he'd have shown his own book, and said he was taking it away to make further alterations . . .

I was hopelessly behind with my work. So I thought, 'sauce for the goose is sauce for the gander,' and nicked his book in turn. And copied his, just making a few alterations, a few more mistakes . . .

and whipped them both back on to the shelf and got away with it. Or so I thought.

Until the homework was passed back. The little blonde Latin mistress kept three books to the end. Then put her hand on them, looked around the class with her gold-rimmed spectacles glinting, like a triumphant Gestapo officer, and said, 'We have a very nasty case of cheating, here. All three books have the same mistake, "the *creamy* foam" when it should have been "the *milk-white* foam".' Then she snapped, 'Stand up, Berry, Donaldson and Stella France'

Stella stood up, very pale. She seemed to sway for a second, then squared her shoulders.

'I have not been copying,' she said, quietly but clearly. Then she turned and looked at me. The same look Jesus Christ must have given Judas Iscariot.

'Well, *I've* not been copying,' said Berry. 'Everyone knows I'm a genius at Latin.' That got a big laugh from the lads. Stella was not popular; she was too good at Latin, and her homework was always in on time. I could see their point of view. She was always a bit bossy, thought a lot of herself, holier than thou.

'I'm taking these books to the head,' said the Latin mistress. 'I'll leave him to deal with it.' And swept out, her pert little nose in the air.

Stella France walked across to me. 'I knew you were *low*,' she said. 'I didn't know you were *that* low.' Her eyes were blazing. 'That's the second time you've ruined my chance of becoming a prefect.' Then she too swept out.

'Ah, love's young dream,' shouted Berry, and all the lads broke out laughing.

I was beating his head against a post of the bike sheds when who but the headmaster should come along, walking to his car. The first thing the head did was to send the interested crowd of small boys away. The second was to say, 'I hope neither of you were hoping for a prefectship, next year? I think you'd better come to my office. Go and wash yourselves first.'

We stood in front of his desk, surveying the worn pattern of the hearth-rug and hating each other.

'What a coincidence,' said the head. 'I just have a report of cheating, involving Berry, Donaldson and Stella France, and now I have a not very inspiring pugilistic display, by Berry and Donaldson. Have the thieves fallen out?'

'I copied off Berry,' I said, sullenly.

'Honesty seems to have returned to you, after some absence,' said the head. 'Still, better late than never. Berry?'

'He's cut my lip,' said Berry. 'He made my nose bleed. I didn't start it.'

'I was thinking more of the state of your soul than your body, Berry,' said the head sharply. 'Have you anything to say to me?'

Berry, the fool, just shuffled. The head looked down at the three exercise books. 'Miss France seems to have made only one error. You have made ten, Berry. It does not seem to me that Miss France was in any need of help from you.'

'It was only a bit of fun,' said Berry. 'A bit of a joke, like.'

'Miss France did not regard it as a joke. I have had her here in tears. She protests her innocence . . . what else have *you* got to say for yourself, Donaldson?'

'I only copied off Berry,' I said again. I mean, you might beat a bloke to pulp, but you don't split on him to the head.

'So I would presume, then, that you, Berry, copied from Miss France by stealing her book from the shelf outside the staffroom?'

Berry said nothing.

'It is not my habit to cane sixth-formers,' said the head. 'But if it happens again . . . off you go, Berry. A word, Donaldson.'

I just stood. I was grasping for a good phrase, that he would like. I didn't fancy the cane either.

'It was an affair of honour, sir.'

He smiled, thinly. 'It looked more like a bar-room brawl to me. Still, I would regard you as being only . . . misguided, Donaldson. Do you think you could find Miss France's house, on your way home? She might like to hear the news. But have a try at washing your face and hands again first. I don't want her mother complaining. And get that blazer sewn up by the morning. At the moment, you look like one of the more unfortunate rejects from Ralph Gardener.' Ralph Gardener was the secondary modern; he uttered the words as he might have uttered 'public lavatory'.

And then, by God, he smiled at me.

Stella came to the door herself, but her mother was just behind.

'Berry confessed. I beat him up. I copied off him. I didn't know it was your book he had. The head knows all about it.'

'You look a real fright,' she said. But she said it with a smile. 'Come in for a cup of tea.'

It was different; it was snug. We weren't in the sitting-room, pretending to be posh. We were in the kitchen, sitting round the fire, drinking out of mugs and eating chocolate biscuits. Even with my loose and bloody tooth they tasted great. And everyone had stopped *pretending*. It was just like being at home. I got chatting to Stella's mother about my future plans, our dog and his funny tricks, my dad's greenhouse, anything. I made her laugh; she had a nice generous laugh, when she came off it. She was a very attractive woman, even if she was about thirty-seven. As pretty as Stella, except for a few wrinkles round her mouth. My mum wasn't any older than her, but my mum wasn't at all glamorous; she was just a mum. Funny. I supposed it went with the posh semi, and all their family still playing tennis at the grand private club at Tynemouth, not just Stella. I mean, I didn't play tennis too badly, but my mum and dad wouldn't know one end of a racket from the other . . .

Anyway, there was I making Stella's mum laugh her head off (I always got on better with girls' mums than girls, all my life), when in walks Stella's father, in his RAF uniform, home on leave from Germany.

I had gathered from Stella that he wasn't a fighter pilot or anything, but he still looked pretty glamorous too. I mean, the glory of the Few still hung around all the RAF in those days. He was a very young-looking, good-looking guy, not worn and grey-haired like my dad.

'Hello,' he said, sizing me up, and not caring much for the torn blazer and bits of leaf and soil in my hair.

Then her mum said, 'You must forgive George, he's been doing battle for your daughter's honour.' So he had to hear all about it, and when he realised there was no sex involved, just cheating at Latin, he turned very jovial, and even asked what I meant to do when I left university. But I didn't hang around long, because the bloke hadn't been home for six months, and I felt like an intruder.

But I had my reward. Because Stella's best friend, Betty Moffatt, went round with my best friend, Tony Stephenson. And Tony told me that Betty had told him that Stella had told her that she liked me much better than she used to, and wouldn't mind if I asked her to go out to the pictures one Saturday night . . . so I told Tony to tell Betty to tell Stella that I might just do that, and one day, walking home for lunch, I did.

'Like to go to the pictures on Saturday? There's a good film on at the Prince's. *The Lost Moment*, starring Robert Cummings and Susan Hayward.'

She opened her pretty lips to say 'yes' and then the awful realisation struck her. I had asked her to go to the Prince's and not the Carlton. And the Carlton was where the sixth form mob went on a Saturday night. It had a row of double seats at the back, that were bookable in advance, and the property of the established couples in the sixth. The row in front was occupied by the likes of Berry, making rude remarks.

But I had asked her to the Prince's, which was posher, and where the grown-ups went.

I was not acknowledging her publicly in front of her friends. I would not face up, for her sake, to the cracks about Fatty France and Fatty Donaldson, and how difficult two fat people would find it to do *It*. I loved her, but was ashamed of my love . . .

But she must have had some feelings for me, because she just tightened her lips and stared straight in front of her and said, 'All right. What time?'

There was a procedure in the cinema in those days; once they put the lights out. The girl gently leaned against the boy. At this signal, he put his arm round her, or at least draped it along the back of the double seat in the back row of the Carlton. If she liked this, she leaned a bit harder. He grabbed her by the top of her far arm. She leaned her head on his shoulder, if she wanted to be kissed. He kissed her. Repeat the prescription ad infinitum. If it didn't go well, all the bloke got was a stiff arm, and all the girl got was a stiff neck.

But we were in the middle of the Prince's cinema, in single seats with a great big seat-arm between us, and all around us were middle-aged adults, who rattled bags of sweeties and hissed deadly threats to make their kids shut up, and who were not above poking you in the back if your two heads close together blocked their view.

We did nothing except watch the picture, which was a boring one about some old dear alone with her memories. Once our knees touched by accident, and both our knees jumped away simultaneously, as if we'd developed St Vitus' Dance. I kept squinting sideways at her Ingrid Bergman profile; in the flickering grey light of the black-and-white projector, she looked as cold and remote as the mountains of the moon.

We walked home in total silence. Neither of us could think of anything to say. I was filled with a kind of dreary sadness. I just knew then I would never in all my life fall in love properly.

The following Monday, she was not in school. I got in a silly panic that she might be ill. That she might be in some decline because I'd taken her to the Prince's and not the Carlton . . . I got into such a panic that I decided to call at her house after school to ask how she was.

When I knocked on the door, her father opened it. He was still in his RAF uniform, but didn't look so grand, because he had his tunic off and you could see his black braces; I always thought braces very vulgar; my father and I always wore belts instead.

He looked pretty harassed, too, and not at all pleased to see me. I became certain then that Stella was suffering from some mysterious female ailment, because I'd taken her to the wrong cinema; and that she had told him all. He was so upset that his RAF regulation Brylcreem hairstyle had fallen apart all over his head in greasy strands, and he looked younger and not at all handsome.

'Who is it, dear?' called Mrs France from the lounge, through the open door. Her voice sounded a bit upset too.

'It's the Donaldson boy,' he said, as if he might be saying, 'It's a case of bubonic plague'.

'Tell him Stella's not well.' Then her voice changed, and she said, 'No, send him in here.'

So in I was marched, in double-quick RAF style. Her mother did look pale and shaken. Sort of guilty and quivery. But she looked me in the eye, with a brave attempt at a smile, and said: 'Stella's been rather upset today. Would you like to go up and see her?'

I almost said, 'No, I'd rather panic and run home, thanks,' but her father was standing behind me now, blocking the way and breathing down my neck.

'He might make her see sense,' said her mother to her father.

'Someone her own age,' said her father to her mother, quite without hope.

'She's up in her bedroom,' said her mother. 'She won't come down. She won't even speak to us, through the door. She's locked it.'

'It's the second on the right,' said her father. 'Just beyond the bathroom.'

I used the bathroom first. I was feeling scared, but also hot and tingly inside. I'd never been in a girl's bedroom before, except when I got lost looking for the toilet at Aunt Florrie's Christmas party, and then her daughter's bedroom was empty, and her daughter looked like Dracula anyway. Then I knocked.

'Go away,' said Stella. You could tell from the way she said it that she had said it a large number of times already. Also, that she'd been crying. I wondered whether she'd be properly dressed, or only all dishevelled in a long nightie, like Freda Curry in the school production of *Macbeth*.

'It's me,' I said.

'Oh!' She did sound totally taken aback.

'Can I come in?'

Long silence. Then she said, 'I'll have to talk to somebody, or I'll go mad. Can you keep a secret?'

'Yeah,' I said firmly, wondering whether I could or not.

I heard very soft footsteps, and the snib on her door went click, and the door opened.

She was sadly, wearing a skirt and blouse, just like normal. But her feet were bare, and her fair hair all dishevelled like Freda Curry's in *Macbeth*; it looked like she'd spent all day running her hands through it. The room smelled all warm and female and excitingly private; I wondered in what direction girls went mad when they did go mad. She hadn't bothered to make her bed, and the hem of a pale blue nightie stuck out from under the pillow, and the bed was strewn with wet lace-edged hankies.

'You might as well sit down,' she said. 'Oh, on the bed, don't be stupid. Haven't you ever seen an unmade bed before?' Then she snibbed the door shut again.

I felt trapped. I felt like General Custer in the closing moments of Custer's Last Stand. Except he had a gun to shoot with.

I decided to take the bull by the horns, when she began to make starting-to-cry noises.

'Are you preggers? Do they know it's not me?' The shadows of a wretched clerking job at Smith's Dock were starting to close around me again. The bloke who had got Pat Shore, belle of the sixth, pregnant was now married to her and working in the office at Smith's Dock, and after the baby she'd lost all her good looks as well . . . and was seen all over town, growing fat and pushing a pram, looking as old as thirty.

'How gallant,' she said sarcastically. I somehow knew then she wasn't preggers. She sounded too dangerous.

'What, then? You're not scared of the summer exams . . .'

'It's not *me* who's pregnant,' she said, viciously.

'Who then? Freda Curry, Millicent Hardy, Minnie Ball?' I ran quickly through her select little bunch of tennis-playing friends, wondering which of my luckless male acquaintances had scored a goal for United in the wrong net.

She took a deep breath, as if she was about to dive into Tynemouth swimming pool off the high board, and said, 'My mother.'

'Who got your mother pregnant?' I mean, I was so totally flabbergasted, I didn't know what I was saying.

I think she nearly hit me. 'My *father*, stupid. Who do you think?'

'That's all right, then!'

'All *right*? Are you *insane*?' Her voice rose to the sort of scream Freda Curry had used for Lady Macbeth in the bloody hands scene, and then cracked. 'How would you like Bill Berry to know your parents still did *it*?'

'What?'

'*It*, you fool. How would you like Bill Berry making remarks about *your* parents doing it?'

'But all our parents did it, or we wouldn't be here . . . even Berry's parents. Or maybe they found him hatching out in the sun on the corporation tip.'

'But that was years ago, before we were born. Berry will know that my parents are doing it *now*. Still. When they're *old*.'

She burst out into a sea of wild weeping, and groped for my hand. Hers was hot and sticky, and I didn't really fancy it, but started squeezing it automatically, like you do with the rind of the half-time orange, during a tense rugger match.

'I shall have to leave school,' she wailed. 'I shall leave home. I shall leave town. I shall go and live with my Aunt Gladys at Consett and work in a shop.'

I was appalled. Working in a shop in Consett was worse, much worse, than a wretched clerking job at Smith's Dock. It was worse than the French Foreign Legion.

'But what about your A levels? What about university?'

'I shall never go to university now. My life is *ruined*.'

I couldn't think of anything helpful to say. I mean, as far as I could see, her life *was* ruined. I began to worry in case my mother got pregnant, too. I should have to *kill* Berry, if she did. And hang for it. Unless the judge thought killing Berry was an act of public service. But Berry's parents wouldn't think so . . . perhaps they were even quite fond of Berry, in a mistaken sort of way.

Stella snatched her hand away. 'Fat lot of help you're being,' she said. She sounded so desperate that she might start screaming or crying or lashing out at me at any moment. So I said, 'I could beat up Berry for you. If he said anything.'

'And all the other boys? And the *girls*? They're a lot worse than Berry, you know! Only they don't shout out what they think. They *whisper*.'

'What about just carrying on? Nobody might notice . . .'

'In a couple of months, my mother will be *enormous*. Besides, she's *proud* of what they've done. She wants to tell everybody.'

'You could get a transfer to Whitley Bay Grammar . . .'

'Half our family live in Whitley Bay. I've got two cousins at school there. *Female* cousins. Don't you know how females gossip?'

'You could make it into a joke, a bit of a laugh . . .'

She gave me such a look I was sure she was going to hit me. I hadn't realised females were physically dangerous when upset.

'Joke? *How*, you great genius? Tell me that.'

Just then I had a brainwave, of sorts. I do have them sometimes.

'Has your mother got a green ration card yet?' Mothers-to-be got issued with special green ration cards which entitled them to stuff like orange juice and rose-hip syrup for free.

'Yes . . . so . . .?' She was still ready to hit me.

'You could take it to school, wave it around in class, make people think that *you* were pregnant. Then, when they were all up to their ears in scandal, you could reveal it wasn't you, just your mother. They'd be so let down, they'd just shut up. You'd have had the laugh on them.'

Again, she was silent a very long time. To keep myself sane, I stared around the room. The wallpaper had yellow Easter bunnies all over it, with ribbons round their necks, from when she was a little kid, before the War. I began studying the bunnies' faces, giving them names. One or two looked stupid, and the rest downright evil. Dangerous things, Easter bunnies. Then I noticed, over the back of the chair, a pair of nylons and a suspender belt. The suspender belt fascinated me like a snake fascinates an Easter bunny . . .

Finally she said, in a very different voice, a voice low and quiet, but no longer despairing, 'It might work. I can't think of anything better. But *when*?'

'Puggy Anderson's lesson. Lower sixth discussion group.'

'Oh, you genius! And you'll back me up? You're good at discussion groups.'

'Yeah. And I'll hit Berry too, if I have to.'

She flung her arms round my neck. She was all warm and damp and it was quite wonderful. Like nothing that ever happened to me before. Even better than me getting my place on the First XV. It was quite a long time before we broke it up; we only did so when we heard doors quietly opening, and footsteps, downstairs. The parents were getting nervous, going on the prowl.

She opened her bedroom door and called downstairs: 'Yes?'

'We were wondering if George would like a cup of tea,' called her mother, very nervously.

'Down in five minutes,' Stella called, almost gaily. Then she gave me a last, damp, warm kiss and let me watch her putting on her make-up, and combing her hair. Somehow, it felt quite a privilege.

When her parents realised she had calmed down, and had no more intentions of doing anything disastrous, they looked at me as if I were God. I was very popular in that house after that, right till the end. Even after the end, her mother used to smile at me sympathetically when we met in the street.

Everyone in the school called him Puggy Anderson, except his immediate close circle of sixth form lads, and they called him Ted. Only behind his back, of course. To his face, we always called him sir. Oh, blessed Pug, what a wonder he was! He was a graduate, but had taught all his working life in the hell of secondary moderns until, at the age of fifty, he came to us. He was so happy to come to us, his grammar-school heaven, that he was content to teach all the rotten lessons the other teachers didn't want. Fourth year RE; first year Latin; Civics right through the school (that child of the Labour Government that everyone hated); how a Town Hall works (as if anyone in their right mind ever wanted to know how a Town Hall works) . . . And Pug took all the sixth form discussion periods as well.

Why he was nicknamed Pug, I shall never know. He had a dark balding head and long nose, and looked Jewish, though he was Scottish. Nobody ever looked or acted less like a Pug. Perhaps that's why people called him that. Nicknames are perverse.

The power of Pug was that he was a great listener. In our discussion group, he put his elbow on the table, and his dark balding head on his hand and just *listened*. But we soon noticed that if we made a good point, either left or right wing, he nodded appreciatively. And if we made a bad point, he would just wince, and draw in his lips, as if he'd bitten on a lemon. How we watched for that nod or that wince; how he ruled us by them! He was never shocked at what we said, provided we said it politely and in good debating manner. Even when we passed a resolution condemning Mr Churchill and Mr Truman as war criminals, for the atom-bombing of Hiroshima and Nagasaki.

Anyway, as we were settling in the library for his lesson, Stella produced the green ration book. It nearly had the effect of an atomic bomb, because everyone knew what it was. The girls began nudging each other, mouthing questions down the long tables, with eyebrows raised so high they almost vanished into their hair. They nearly went mad.

As for Berry and his cronies . . . for once they were silenced, at the magnitude of the disaster. Even for them, to lose your chance of going to university was like a death, and no girl who'd had a baby *ever* went on to university.

Pug was fiddling with some papers, getting ready for a discussion of British colonial policies in East Africa. So he didn't see at first.

It was only when Berry, recovering his wits and his usual charm of speech, yelled to Stella, 'Who's the father?' that Pug realised something was going on.

Stella gave a lovely, demure, contented smirk and called back, 'My father.' She played it beautifully. At the idea of incest, even Berry went into a tail-spin. A deathly hush fell over the whole room. They were faced with a horror so great . . .

'What have you got there, Stella?' asked Pug kindly; though he swallowed and licked his lips as he waited for her answer.

'A green ration book,' she responded with a gleeful grin, shameless woman.

'*Whose* ration book, Stella?' Oh, poor, kind Pug, he was visibly breaking out into a sweat.

'My mother's, sir!'

Such an 'Oh' of relief came from the girls. Such an enormous roar of relieved laughter came from the boys.

'She had you fooled there, Berry!'

'You really fell for it, didn't you?' People punched him in the back unmercifully, while he tried to hide his rage behind a sick grin.

Suddenly, having a pregnant mother was smart, the thing to do. All the girls, being potential Geordie matriarchs at heart, were dead keen to know all about the coming baby. All the lads were glad that Berry had been made such a fool of. And dear Pug, crafty as ever, led us into a discussion on the new Welfare State and told us of the little kids who'd had rickets before the war because they were born to half-starved mothers. Their poor little bowed legs and caved-in chests . . . it was one of the best discussion groups we ever had. And Berry never raised the topic again.

Now came the calm time, the happy time. I was round at Stella's house a lot; she even began to improve my Latin properly, because we did our unseens together and she was a good teacher, and I wasn't a fool. I became almost part of the family. They took me down to the posh tennis club as their guest, and Stella and I reached the semi-finals of the all-schools mixed doubles that summer holiday. Stella even came to our house for tea, and my dad showed her his greenhouse and tomato plants, which was practically his equivalent of bestowing the

Nobel Prize on a female. By the new autumn term, my behaviour had improved so much that when Stella got her full prefect's badge, they even made me a sub-prefect, though it didn't come down to anything more dynamic than stamping a lot of books in the school library.

The baby got itself born, and Stella used to greet me at the door carrying it in her arms, which I found curiously moving, even if it did dribble down her cardigan. One day, it would be her turn to have a baby; and mine, if I was still around. But only after we'd been to university together and . . . it was too far off to worry about. But I just had this happy, calm feeling that all our lives we'd be going on together, side by side. I used to go on long walks, just to feel happy about it.

And so that long term passed, and the contentment and happiness that it seemed might last for ever. And then the snow came, and with it, the end.

It was on the last day of the autumn term. School broke up at half past two, after a carol service when for once everyone sang with all their hearts. Then the girl prefects invited us across to their prefects' room for all manner of cream cakes and pop in glasses, including even shandy. There was a lot of quiet arm-in-arm hugging by the couples, which tended to block the circulation in that confined space, but nobody minded; and, under rather artistic paper hats, made by Freda Curry in the art room, some surprising people kissed other surprising people. The only thing that spoiled it was that Berry turned up, even though he wasn't a prefect, though most of his mates were. But it was

Christmas, and at Christmas I was prepared even to put up with Berry, fool that I was.

Afterwards, the Head Girl made a surprise announcement. They had planned a snowball fight for us. We would go to a disused pit-heap just beyond the school playing-field, and there we would take even sides, half boys, half girls, and have our fight. The girls were pleased with themselves; they thought they were being very daring and emancipated; they were pretty high and full of themselves and flirty, draping skeins of tinsel round the boys' hair and laughing at the absurd effect.

We set off in a long gaggle through the gathering dusk, lots of quiet hugging going on. Most of us were paired off with some girl by this time, and I think all the rest had hopes that night. There must have been about forty of us, half boys, half girls.

We hauled them up the steep sides of the pit-heap with great shows of strength. None of the girls had been there before, but all the lads knew it well from when they were young. As a savage place, a place outside society, where gangs fought with stones and sticks, and many a bloody nose resulted. A place of twisted arms and split lips. Not an evil place exactly, but a hard and merciless place. But the girls were enchanted by it; it looked like a miniature mountain under snow; and, stretched out beneath it, the lights of the town twinkled in pretty skeins, and our industrial ruins became fairyland. A far-away fairyland. On top, it was lonely, and the wind blew cold and harsh, and Stella beside me clutched the lapels of her school raincoat together with one mittened hand. Her mittens had yellow flowers embroidered on the back, I remember.

And here was the Head Girl again, her cheeks red and rosy, prettily bossy with her neat chignon of blonde hair and her little clipboard with the chosen sides listed on it. We gathered around and she began to read out the names.

And then Berry grabbed Audrey Chalmers, and began stuffing a snowball down the back of her neck. And Audrey Chalmers, the silly cow, one of those girls of whom it was rumoured long ago that they let lads do things in the dark of the playing-field, began half-screaming and half-laughing, half-struggling and half-enjoying it.

The Head Girl gave Berry a nasty look. 'D'you mind? I'm trying to read out the sides.'

'We know the sides already,' shouted Berry. 'One side is the boys, and the other is the girls. Get them, lads! Fix 'em proper! Stuck-up cows! *Show* them!'

And two of his cronies grabbed the Head Girl and began shoving snow down her neck. And suddenly she was screaming as well.

It just happened. I wouldn't have believed it possible, with so many happy settled couples, but it just happened. In a second girls were lying on the ground, writhing and showing great and sexy expanses of thigh while the boys bent over them stuffing freezing snow into every opening available. It was a kind of madness.

And I was just as guilty as all the rest.

I think at the beginning, some of the girls were half-enjoying it. But not for long. The giggles and protests died, and only the screaming, higher in pitch, remained. Except for one or two girls, the Head Girl among them, who fought like demons, fought with fists and nails; and there was blood running down Berry's cheek.

And then it was all over, and there was only a wretched, stumbling, falling, sliding, retreat of girls, straggling down the trampled, defiled, white snow of the pit heap. And the sound of real sobbing coming back up to us, shocking and unbelievable, as we stood on the trampled top, amongst the girls' discarded scarves and single gloves and even a snow-boot, lying like dead animals in the snow.

The girls gathered in a crowd at the bottom, and stared up at us. And we stared silently down at them. Some were hugging companions who were really hysterical. I think it was the first time I'd heard girls really hysterical.

The Head Girl's voice came up clearly; she was a leader still.

'I think you are all *despicable*. I shall see the headmaster hears about this.'

'It was your idea,' shouted Berry. 'Can't you take a bit of fun?'

'Fun? Some of my girls are really *hurt*. Wait till their fathers hear.'

There was an uneasy stirring among the boys. 'You've shit it, Berry. You've really shit it now.'

'You blaming *me*?' Berry shouted back. 'You were all doing it. You enjoyed it. Why blame me?'

'We want our gloves and scarves back,' called the Head Girl from below. 'Or have you turned into thieves as well?'

'If you want them, come and fetch them,' shouted Berry. But Tony and I, and one or two more of the decent lads, began picking them up. I went down the side of the tip, sliding dangerously, with my arms laden.

But if I expected thanks, or even a lessening of the hate, I was sadly mistaken. I tried making little jokes; just speaking to the girls. But they just grabbed their snowy, trampled things in silence, and put them on. Nobody looked at me. Except Stella, who was standing beside the Head Girl.

'Sorry,' I said to her, with a weak, lopsided grin. 'It *was* just a bit of fun, really.'

'You sound just like Berry,' she said, tight-lipped. But what else would she dare say, with all the other girls looking at her like that? I'd walk her home. She'd be different once I got her on her own . . .

But she wasn't. She just stalked along silently, so fast I had to practically run to keep up with her.

'Look,' I said, finally grabbing her by the shoulder and swinging her round to face me. 'It's me. Remember?'

'Oh, yes, I remember,' she said. 'Take your hands off me. I don't belong to you. Not any more.'

'But . . .' I said.

'If you tell me again it was only a bit of fun, I swear I'll hit you. I'm soaked to the skin, my stockings are ruined and they're the last decent pair I had. I wore them specially for today. Both my knees are scraped and my shoulder hurts like hell.'

'It wasn't me that did that to you.'

'And you didn't try and stop them. You were too busy stuffing snow down Judy Falconer's bra.'

It's funny how girls still notice things and get jealous.

'Look – we've had our ups and downs . . .'

'This down is permanent. I never want to see you again.'

'But what about your New Year party?'

'I'm cancelling my New Year party. I'll take the girls to the pictures instead . . .'

'But what about *us* – you and me?'

'*Stuff* you and me.' There were tears in her eyes.

'I'll *kill* Berry,' I said. 'It was all his fault. He must have been plotting it for days.'

'Kill Berry by all means. Let me know by postcard when you've done it. But it won't change anything. Do you think I could ever trust you again, after that?'

'What do you think I am?' Now I was shouting, hysterical.

'I know what you are. A so-called man.'

'But I'm not a man. I'm *me*.'

'Oh, no, you had your chance to be "me" on the pit-heap. You were just one of the boys, instead. And don't tell me you don't know what came over you. That's what the SS said at Nuremburg. And don't *whinge*. If men aren't bullying, they're whingeing.'

'Look, I'm sorry.'

'Too late, George. It was good, while it lasted. Thanks for the good times.' And she gave a weary little smile, that foolishly still led me to hope, then turned away, up her road.

'I'll see you again,' I shouted after her.

And of course I did. In the classroom, on the way home, even at prefects' meetings. It even got so she would speak to me again. Until I tried an appeal. Then she just turned to stone.

I saved my final quarrel with Berry until the day we all left school. I beat him to a pulp, but it didn't change anything.

The next time she saw me she said, 'I heard. Don't bother to send me a postcard.'

And that was the last time I ever saw her.

I still think about her, every day.

First Death

They stood on the cliff-top, killer and victim. Neither knew yet what they were going to become.

The moon, riding high, breasting the wind-driven rags of cloud without difficulty, shone on them. The boy was tall and burly; the girl tall and slim. Both had long hair that blew in the wind, as if freshly washed. But hers was longer. Both wore long fawn raincoats that flapped strongly round their legs, as they hugged each other close.

Under the moon, the white uneven bars of great waves stretched to the lost horizon; broken only by the ruler-straight lines of the piers which protected the harbour. At the end of each mile-long pier, a lighthouse winked. Between lighthouse and shore, white explosions of foam rubbed out sections of the piers for a moment; then the ruler-straight piers would surface again.

'Let's walk out to the lighthouse,' he said. 'We've got plenty of time before the bus goes.'

She drew in her breath sharply, and shuddered.

'It's OK,' he said. 'I've done it dozens of times, ever since I was a kid. I'll look after you.'

She watched the breaking waves in horror, for a long moment. But she was at the beginning of love. Finally she said, 'OK, then,' taking his hand and pulling his arm tighter round her, as if it was a scarf.

Still clasped together, they descended.

He was exultant. How often he had walked this pier in the dark and storm? Alone. Dreaming of the girl that would come, who would walk it with him. And now she was here, her slim waist inside his enclosing arm. She was taller than he had dreamed her, almost too tall for a girl. And she laughed too often for his liking, a sudden loud nervous laugh. But she was here, solid, real, all his. He would never have to walk this pier alone in the dark again. No more dark, desperate moods, when he thought of death coming.

Instead he heard the great wave coming; the great seventh wave that would swallow the pier.

'Down,' he shouted. 'Close behind the wall.' And dragged her down, though he felt the new willingness in her body. The wave exploded up over their heads, with a sound like a depth-charge. Then showered down, too heavy for rain, on the far edge of the pier. She screamed at the towering giant, then laughed breathlessly as it passed safely overhead, leaving them dry as a bone.

'You *clever* old thing,' she said.

'You just have to listen,' he said, with grave mock-modesty, stuffing down his exultation. 'The big one makes quite a different sound. It *rumbles.*'

'Why does it rumble?'

'It picks up boulders from the sea-bed and throws them at the pier. It's wearing the pier away. Slowly. In another hundred years, this pier won't be here. They'll have to build a new one.'

'Go on,' she said saucily. 'Pull the other leg, it's got bells on it.'

He thought of her long, beautiful legs, which he'd only seen when they played tennis. But it was only a blurred, warm, fleeting thought. For he was a nice young man, an innocent. He thought much more of her huge grey eyes than of her legs. He had no plans for her legs, such as an older man might have had. All his planning went into writing her long poems that did not rhyme, and which she did not fully understand, though she kept them, and stored them in her sweet-smelling handkerchief drawer; under the handkerchiefs where her mother wouldn't find them.

'It doesn't pick up boulders,' she said accusingly. 'There's no boulders on the sea-bed round here. It's all mud.'

'The boulders are from the old pier, the one the waves broke. The one my grandfather helped to build. It broke in the great storm of 1918. Then they had to build this one. Those boulders used to be square, but now they're round, where the seas have worn them away. It's like a mincing machine out there. If anyone fell over this wall, on a stormy night, they wouldn't just drown. They'd be ground up to fish-food. They'd never find your body.'

She shuddered inside his arm and said, 'I don't believe you. You're having me on.' Then in her next breath she said, 'I want to *see*.' And leaned across the three foot wide top of the granite wall, peering down into the dark.

'Christ, you'll fall,' he yelled in a panic, a panic that convinced her he was telling the truth.

'Hold on to my legs then. I have to *see*.' Feeling safe with his strong grip on her legs, she wriggled further out still. Till she could lower her head beyond the wall, and see the tossing ghostly maelstrom of foam below.

'Look out,' he shouted. 'Another big wave coming.' And heaved her legs backwards, so they fell in a heap at the base of the wall, as the next great wave passed over them. They went on lying there, while she gave him a long warm closed-mouth innocent kiss. Her lips were a mixture of warm and icy, with the taste of salt on them. They lay there kissing while two more great waves passed overhead. Finally she broke off, breathless, and said, 'You told me the truth. I saw the foundations of the old pier. It sticks out at an angle from this one.'

'That's right, it does.' They kissed a long last time. Then she got up, all practical and slightly cross. 'I hope you haven't got my raincoat dirty. My mother will go *mad*.'

He peered at her coat dubiously in the dim waxing and waning light of the moon. 'You'll be OK. The sea washes everything clean out here.'

'Better had. If Mummy found dirt on my coat, God knows what she'd think we'd been up to.' They were both silent for a moment, thinking about that, then he said, 'Same as she did, when she was your age.'

'Mummy's not like that.'

'Everybody's like that,' he said, greatly daring. He had never met her mother. Or her father.

'C'mon,' she said. 'Let's walk, or we'll miss the last bus.'

They walked fast now, hand in hand. She swung his arm strongly, backwards and forwards, in time with their walking. As if she was working off some emotion he couldn't understand.

At first, the lighthouse at the end of the pier just winked at them. Three quick flashes, then a darkness, then two more, then darkness again. But as they got nearer, and the lighthouse began to loom over them, the flashes began to turn into circling beams of light passing over their heads.

She stopped, gazing up, entranced. 'It's like a great wheel,' she said. 'A great circling wheel of light. Just for us.'

He squeezed her hand, immensely pleased with her. In his mind she had passed another test. She understood. She was worthy. She was the inheritor of all his childhood; all the lonely nights he'd walked this pier, waiting for her to come. He gave her, without saying a word, the whole kingdom of his lonely heart.

As if she sensed it, she shivered. 'Hug me tight,' she said, self indulgently. 'Poor Sheila's cold.'

He hugged her as tight as he could, standing between her and the cold wind from the sea, pulling her against him hard, wrapping the end of his long student scarf round her graceful neck. She grabbed his spare hand, and plunged both entwined hands into the depths of her raincoat pocket, where there was a slight patch of warmth.

They were silent again, each enjoying the little illusion of a dwelling-place they had made. Then she said, 'There are so many lighthouses flashing. All along the coast, both ways.'

'To the south there's Marden Rock, then Sunderland, the slow yellow one. Slow, slow, quick, quick, slow. Up north, there's St Mary's Island, then Blyth. It's like they're talking to each other, in the dark.'

'How d'you know them all?'

'My grandad taught me, when I was about three. First time he brought me along here. On his shoulders . . .' He wondered what his grandfather would have made of her. A fine big lass, he would have said.

Just then, as if his kingdom approved of her, was having a celebration in her honour, a ship's siren sounded from further up the river. White lights, red lights, green lights; strong lights, moving across the still, starry constellation that was the distant street lights of the port.

'Ship coming out. Let's see her pass.'

'Have we got time?'

'Bags of time.' The idea of having a ship leave harbour, and not seeing it pass was unbearable to him. None of his family could have done it.

They waited. The black bulk with its brilliant lights grew huge. Across the water, they could hear the monstrous thudding of its engine, and the swish of its propellors, hurling up a constant fountain of fluorescent green at the stern.

'She's empty. High in the water.'

'Oh, I wish we were aboard her . . . going somewhere.'

He thought of being with her, in some dimly lit, mahogany-lockered cabin, with the swinging oil-lamp turned low. Then crushed the thought back down again, for he was a nice young man. Instead, he said gruffly, 'You'd be pretty seasick tonight, I reckon. Look.'

And as they watched, the ship reached the end of the shelter of the piers, and the first wave took her, and she suddenly pitched like a bucking bronco, the mast-lights swinging wildly in circles.

'Oh, now you've spoilt it,' she said. 'You're *horrid*.' And she gave him a last long lingering kiss, to prove to him how horrid he was.

It was a long exhausting run back; they just caught the last bus as it was pulling out; feeling sick and gasping.

The last time they came, only the darkness was the same. The moon was gone, the fog was down, the foghorn on the lighthouse mourned like a lost spirit, calling to other lost spirits that called back faintly through the heavy grey blanket. Out in the harbour, the bell-buoy tolled like a funeral bell. As they passed a streetlamp, he saw the fog had gathered like beads of dew on the ends of Sheila's dark hair.

She'd been in a funny mood all evening. Her body was as affectionate as ever; more affectionate. Little desperate bursts of cuddling; sudden demands for a kiss, her fingers writhing inside his like desperate little animals. But her mind was far away. Long silences. Sometimes he had to say something to her twice, before she answered.

Outwardly, he tried to stay cheerful; even if none of his new jokes seemed to work, and he had to explain them to her. Inside he was frantic. He had given up his whole world to her; he still did all the things he used to do; college-work, rugby, being at home with the family. But they weren't solid any more; they were just things he did to fill in the time before he could see her again. She was his home now; her body holding him in some dark corner, doorstep, alleyway, bus station.

He had to get her to a place where things would be all right again.

'Let's go along the pier.'

'Oh, I don't feel like it much tonight.'

'*Please*.'

'Oh, all right then.'

But even the pier wasn't all right tonight. The waves were hardly breaking over it at all; no more than a bit of spray that soon they didn't find worth dodging. They had their raincoats. And there were people on the pier. Men walking dogs; other courting couples; who swam at them suddenly out of the darkness, so they could never feel really alone.

They huddled at the pier end, under the great wheel of the light-house, next to the lifebuoy you were supposed to throw if some poor bugger fell in; much good it would do them, even in this sea.

Silence. Then, muffled, he again heard the beat of a heavy engine. Smelled the smell of sooty smoke through the mist, and the smell of kippers cooking.

'Trawler,' he said.

'How d'you know that?' There was none of the old wonder in her voice.

'Can't you smell them cooking their supper? They don't eat kippers on the mail-boat.' He said it with a little scorn, a little anger. Trawler-people were his people. People who went on the mail-boat to Norway, to Stavanger, were her sort of people. Posh holiday-makers. He suddenly wanted to hurt her, because she was hurting him so much.

'Oh,' she said, as if it didn't matter.

Then she said, 'I can't see you any more.' In a dull dead voice.

'Yewhat?' He simply couldn't take in what he was hearing.

'I can't see you any more.'

She was still cuddling him tightly round the waist; hanging on to him for grim death. She was saying one thing and doing another.

'Who says?'

'My father.'

'What does he know about it? He hasn't even *met* me.'

'He doesn't want me to get involved. He says I'm too young.'

'But he let you go out with me before!'

'Oh, he wants me to have boyfriends. He just doesn't want me to get in over my head.'

'In other words, anybody can go out with you except me.'

'Yes, I suppose so.'

A terrible rage swept over him. He seemed to see the face of every other boy in the sixth form he had just left. The faces of the boys at the rugby club; the faces of his own friends. Anyone could have a crack at her; open season. Anyone but him.

He had visions of them pawing at her; taking her up dark corners. He suddenly wanted to smash every one of their faces in.

She said, timidly, 'You haven't got much to worry about. I don't want any of them. It'll take me a long time to get over you.'

'You still love me then?' She nodded mutely, so he could tell there were tears running down her face, even though, in the fog, he couldn't see them.

'How *fucking* stupid.' He never swore in front of her, though he swore a bit elsewhere, so it came out doubly shocking.

'What's he afraid of? That I might rape you or something?'

'Don't.' The word came out as agony.

'Well, what *is* he afraid of, then?' He felt stronger suddenly. As if he had her absent, never-seen father by the throat. While he kept the anger up, his own agony was kept at bay.

'He . . . he wants me to go out with lots of boys. So when I come to choose, I can choose wisely.'

'Are you allowed to choose me?'

She was silent. Suddenly he reached up tenderly to touch her cheek. It was wet with tears. He knew the answer was no.

'No use for trawler-folk, then? My dad's a bloody *skipper*. He owns half his own boat. He could buy your dad out ten times over. What's so bloody marvellous about being the public librarian? What car does he drive?'

'Don't. Please don't.'

'Why not?'

'He is my father.' There was a note of anger, of resistance now, that told him he had gone too far. But he was too full of rage. He wasn't able to stop.

'Christ. I wish now I hadn't taken care of you. I wish I'd taken advantage of you. I wish I'd got you pregnant. He'd have liked a trawler-brat for a grandson. I should have had a go when I had the chance. You'd have let me, wouldn't you?'

She clung to him sobbing now. She was all his again. She said, gulping grotesquely, 'When I'm with him, what he says makes sense. But when I'm with you . . .'

He tried to be reasonable. 'Look, why don't you talk to him, explain to him? Does he know I'm going to college – that I'm going to be a teacher, and a poet? I'd never go on the trawlers. It's a hell of a life. I've seen too much of it. Our Fred's divorced and our Billy's a drunk. I'm not going to get caught like that. I'm going to be different. Maybe I could end up a college lecturer . . .'

'I've explained to him. Till I'm blue in the face. He just says trawler-people are trawler-people, and that's an end to it.'

He could have screamed out loud. He hadn't thought things could hurt any more than they had already. But they could. Now he had betrayed his whole family, his tough, laughing dad, his cheerful, friendly mam. And still it wasn't enough.

'Just what *do* you want?' he screamed at her.

'I just want to go home,' she said.

'Then I'll never see you again! Can I write to you? At the bank? Nobody would know . . .'

'No,' she said, and it was a terrible flat final 'no', like a door slamming. 'No, I'm not going to deceive my father. Not even for you!'

'So it's never again?' Still he couldn't believe it was happening.

'Yes,' she said, wretchedly. 'Never again. You'll get over me, Stan. The world's full of girls.'

'That's what *he* said to you, isn't it? That's what *he* told you to say?'

She hung her head. 'Yes.'

'Everything you've said tonight is what *he* told you to say?'

'Yes.'

'But what do *you* say? Left to yourself? Without him getting at you?'

'Stan – he's my father. He has my best interests at heart. I'm not seventeen yet . . .'

'My mam married my dad when she was seventeen.' A wild idea swam into his head. He grasped it like a drowning man clutches at a straw. 'Look, will you come home with me now? My mam and dad would understand. They'd stand by us. We could get married. I could leave college. I could get a clerking job at Smith's Dock tomorrow! We've got a spare bedroom . . .'

He blundered on into her deepening silence, then stopped in total despair.

'Take me home, Stan,' she said. 'You and daddy – you're tearing me apart. I just can't take any more.' Her voice was so dull, so low, so exhausted that he felt afraid for her, and took her arm, and led her, as if she was a blind person, to the steps that led down from the lighthouse platform to the pier proper.

But as they reached the steps, his gentle mood swung again. She was so weary, passive, that desire for her rocketed through him. He pinned her hard against the wall, kissing her helpless face, struggling to find the buttons of her raincoat. And she just stood, letting him. Only she was slowly unknowingly, sliding along the smooth granite wall; to the place where it dipped, before the steps started. The place where it was really too low for safety; the place that had fascinated him ever since he was a little child. Beyond the curve of her wet cheek, and the swirl of her windblown hair, he could see the creaming, curdling foam of the waves. If they went over the wall now, together, the filthy adult world could never touch them again. They would be for ever free, for ever pure, in the wind and the sea. It seemed inevitable . . .

Till she whispered in his ear, ever so wearily, 'I wouldn't stop you. I don't blame you . . .'

It was a surrender so total, he knew he could win in death.

And thus became convinced he could win in life too. He *had* won. Now it was only a matter of patience. Every year that passed, he would get stronger, and her father would get weaker. It was only a matter of time and patience. He thought confusedly of Patient Griselda and Jacob working to win Rachel. Fourteen years, if that's what it took. He'd work so hard, the years would spin by.

Just in time, he snatched her away from the terrible wall. She gave a tiny laugh and said, 'Yes, I think I would rather live, really.' Then added, 'I think we're both mad.' But she said it proudly.

'C'mon, you're cold. And you'll miss your bus.' Now he had made up his mind, he was absurdly eager to get on with his new life of working and waiting.

But as they passed the dark seat tucked into the corner of the cliff, she drew him in. 'Love me, Stan. For the last time. The way only you can.'

It seemed to him the first fruits of victory. Already she was changing her mind . . . so he said, newly generous, 'You'll miss the bus. What'll your father say?'

'To hell with what he wants, tonight.' And she drew him to her, warmly, taking his head between her hands.

They had to walk all the way to her home. She drew his head to her lips, holding it with both hands, on her very doorstep, which she had never done before. Suppose her father was watching, peeping round a curtain of that still-lit window? To hell with him . . .

That last kiss exceeded anything he had ever known before. It made his head spin.

Then she said, 'Goodbye, Stan,' and was gone through the door with a rattle of her latch-key.

He walked home under the midnight stars, oddly exultant. For a huge poem to her was growing in his mind. He murmured the first line to himself.

A woman is like a city.

He did not see her for three months, as the new spring grew without her. There were times of a strange, almost holy peace. The Sunday mornings wandering through the ruins of the cliff-top priory, while the warm sun melted the hoar-frost on the grass, and he read the tombstones of those who were past all earthly pain and found them good and comforting companions. And new poems to her sprang into his head unbidden, without effort. His college magazine was going to print three of them. His professor got to see them, and praised their vividness, while carping about their metre . . .

And there were dark times, when he wandered alone along the pier through wilder storms than he had ever taken her through; storms when the pier safety-gates were shut to exclude the public, and he had to climb round them, hanging out over the raging rumbling waves. Storms that soaked him to the skin, carefully though he listened for the approaching rumble of the big wave. Three times he was nearly lifted off his feet and swept away. But always he exulted in the howling dark; for, as the lighthouse flashed its message, he knew that she walked with him in spirit; that, far inland, she would lift her head from her lamplit book and listen to the wind howling in her own chimneys, and would smile to herself, knowing where he would be, and perhaps worrying a little. And there would be nothing her father could do about it, fat smug pig. For the storm was their secret friend, the gale their secret messenger.

When he did see her, out shopping in Saville Street with her mother, she looked pale and weary and bored; a look which made his heart pound in his chest. He thought her mother looked a little fussy stupid woman in her dumpy fur coat.

And then, wonder of wonders, Sheila looked straight at him, as if she had felt his glance stroke her cheek like his hand so often had. And her eyes seemed to leap the whole width of the busy street, in their pain, and stayed fixed on him, till her mother turned and spoke sharply to her, and they went into Marks and Spencer.

He did not try to follow them. Only a glutton and a fool would have wanted more, after that long look of agony and longing.

The Easter holidays came, and the college magazine was published. He bought a spare copy and sent it to the bank, without a covering letter. It was his pride that he had kept his word and not written to her.

The summer term passed, and his exam results amazed even himself. His professor, at the end of year interview, painted a bright future for him. He solved the problem of the long vac by going out working on his father's boat. The fishing was prolific in those days, and the money was good. He loved the movement of the deck under his feet and the kick of spray in his face. He squared his conscience by writing several long vivid poems on the fishing, of which the best was 'Night Fishing'.

Under the glare of lamps, the straining hands
Are weary with rope, sluggish with gutting-knife . . .

He was not a trawlerman; he was a poet working on trawlers. John Masefield had been a sailor . . .

All went well, until that Sunday morning walk along the pier. In that town, everyone walked along the pier on sunny Sunday mornings. Solitary men with excited, pulling dogs and pipes well alight. Whole families, blocking the pier from one side to the other. Pairs of young lovers, whom he watched with a sad, benign tolerance. As he was watching this approaching couple now. Bloke looked a bit of a stuff-shirt in an immaculate blazer, but the girl had nice legs, nearly as good as Sheila's . . .

He looked at the girl's face. He nearly didn't recognized her, for she had had her hair cut short, her beautiful, beautiful hair that he'd longed to run his hands . . . But it was Sheila. And she was laughing. Looking up at the bloke and laughing. They must just be friends . . . son of a friend of her father's. What was the harm in a walk, a laugh?

And then the bloke said something to her, and reached across and took her hand; like he was used to taking it.

Stan tried to stand aside to let them pass, without noticing him. But he half-tripped on an old inlaid rusty ring, and fell against the granite wall. And so of course she saw him.

And among all those smiling bright breezy faces, among all that quiet murmur of Sunday morning enjoyment, their two faces echoed each other in horror, as if they stared at some terrible road accident.

She let go the bloke's hand, and ran to him. A foot apart, they stood trembling.

'It's not what it looks like,' she cried.

'I've got eyes,' he said bitterly.

'Don't . . .' she said.

'Don't what?' It came out in a spit of utter bitterness. 'I'll do what I want. What's it got to do with you?'

'Please . . .'

'C'mon, Sheila,' said the bloke in the blazer, impatiently. 'We haven't got all day. Your parents . . .'

She could not break away. Her horrified eyes stared into his.

'Now look,' said the bloke in the blazer. Stan gave him a stare. His hair was beautifully cut; no local barber for that one. Big, but soft. Probably thought he was tough because he played rugby in winter. Stan could have taken him apart with one hand tied behind his back.

Except the middle of Stan was missing now; he felt gutted, hacked in half and dead, like a kippered herring. He felt doubly gutted.

That she should have this bloke was bad enough: but that she should have brought him to *this* place. Our place. My place. My place ever since I was a kid. The place where I dreamed.

It was Stan who turned and ran, scattering the holidaymakers in his path as if he was a mad thing.

By dark, he was back. The wind was rising, blowing spray in his face, even before he reached the pier itself. He could hear the boom and rumble of the waves before he even reached the safety gates. But, oddly, the gates were still open; maybe the lighthouse people were too busy to close them. He was glad he wouldn't have to climb out past the gates; he couldn't trust his strong trawlerman's hands to hold him safe any more. Not tonight. He felt as weak as a kitten. And he had things to do, before he made an end of it. His pockets were stuffed with poems.

He met one or two people on his way along. They were practically running, driven by the force of the wind. The young couples were enjoying it, laughing and shouting. But the men with dogs were making noises like they'd be glad to be home. One of them said to him, 'Be careful, son.'

And another! 'It's a wild night, hinny.'

But he reached the place; the place where the wall dipped by the stairs; though he often staggered in his new-found weakness. He leaned against the wall for support, and pulled out the first poem. By the revolving wheel of light, he caught a glimpse of the first two lines.

Under the glare of lamps, the straining hands . . .

Then he let go of it, and it whirled up like a startled gull and flew off into the night. Poem after poem followed, as he thought what a fool he'd been. He should have listened all these years to his brothers. One might be divorced, and the other a drunk, but they both knew how to handle women. Catch 'em quick and treat 'em rough. Never give 'em a chance to draw breath. Grab what you want while it's going and run. And never let 'em near man's business . . .

Well, he'd not listened. He'd let her run her hands through all his business, all his soul and she'd chucked him away. There was just nothing left, except painful thoughts that clung to him like the boiling tar he'd once seen cling to a road-mender and burn him, screaming, near to death.

He glanced at the last poem. He knew it off by heart.

You are a land, a sacred land

Where only I may come

A place where I can make my stand

A place that I call home . . .

Then he let it go, and it flew off like all the rest.

Suddenly, it was time to go. He was not afraid of the sea; the sea was clean; the sea washed everything clean . . .

He got one foot up onto the top of the wall with some difficulty; it was not easy against the gusts. He remembered bitterly that it was Plato who'd said that women have no souls. She'd find out if she had a soul or not, when she read about him in the newspaper.

He'd left no note. Nobody would know why he'd done it; except her. And her father.

He was poised, when he heard two voices near. He pulled down his foot again, in a sudden panic. This was a very private thing he was doing; he didn't want any spectators. So he just leaned against the wall; staring out to sea, and listened.

Two men's voices, a bit breathless, but middle-aged and confident.

One said, 'You can't get them for love nor money, you know.'

Love nor money. It was a saying Stan knew well. But he'd only ever thought about love. Money was just something to take her out with to buy her presents.

The other man said, 'I'll settle for money. You got money, you can buy love.'

'Aye, you can buy most things, if you've got money. I never despise a bit of the ready.'

'Bit of the ready? You're loaded, Jack.'

'Don't tell the taxman that. That bugger's after me all the time. I wish I could find a decent accountant. Mine's an incompetent twit.'

'They're all incompetent twits. Take that fool Murray in the Borough Treasurer's office. I showed him where his best interests lay, but he wouldn't listen. We'll have to give him the push, somehow.'

'Aye.'

The two men hadn't noticed Stan yet, as he cowered in the corner by the stair. But he could see their cigars, glowing like stars as each gust of wind hit them, then going back to dull red in the lulls or streaming trails of sparks, as their owners tapped them into the waves.

And he realised he knew the men slightly, from being with his father at the fish-auctions on the quayside. Fish merchants, said to be as rich as Croesus, flicking their bids to the waiting auctioneer with the ends of their cigars, standing amid the rough jerseys and oilskins in their expensive camel coats. And town councillors, too. Talking about getting rid of a public servant.

Her father was a public servant.

Given time, her father could be got rid of. If you knew the right people, and had plenty of the ready . . .

You could say that with the last of his poems, the poet who was Stan had already gone into the sea. The poet was dead. There was no other way of putting it. But his body and mind remained, idly leaning against the pier wall. Listening. Learning to be something new. At which he would become very good, for he was a very bright lad.

Councillor Stan Morstow. S. Morstow and Co, Accountants. County Councillor Stan Morstow, chairman or vice-chairman of nearly all committees, but especially the Libraries and Recreation Committee . . .

It might have been better for all concerned, if the waves had taken his body too.